CRMM

HEART

Theatre Sister Alison Wood is determined to get a job in Parkleigh Hospital's new cardiology unit. But Alison's hopes are dashed when she meets the head of the team—for Greg Verney is not only a brilliant heart surgeon, but he's also the man who jilted her two years ago!

HEART OF A SURGEON

BY

ALEXINA RAWDON

MILLS & BOON LIMITED
15–16 BROOK'S MEWS
LONDON W1A 1DR

*First published in Great Britain 1985
by Mills & Boon Limited*

© Alexina Rawdon 1985

*Australian copyright 1985
Philippine copyright 1985*

ISBN 0 263 74961 4

*Set in 10 on 12 pt Linotron Times
03–0185–52,000*

*Photoset by Rowland Phototypesetting Ltd
Bury St Edmunds, Suffolk
Made and printed in Great Britain by
Richard Clay (The Chaucer Press) Ltd
Bungay, Suffolk*

CHAPTER ONE

SISTER Alison Wood felt a strong sense of exhilaration as she drove her Mini into the car park of Parkleigh Memorial Hospital. It was a bright spring morning, promising a perfect day and that was the reason for her *joie de vivre*. In front of her the sun was making dappled patterns on the grass where it filtered through the fresh green foliage of the chestnut trees which fringed the car park. Bright crocuses peeped their colourful heads through the grass and the well-tended flower beds were rich with daffodils nodding their yellow heads in the soft breeze.

Alison parked her car and then stood looking around for a brief moment, inhaling the scented air and enjoying the quiet beauty of the hospital garden.

She waved to one of the gardeners, who was edging a nearby flower bed. 'Good morning, Fred,' she called. 'Will the weather hold?'

Fred looked up and then shook his head mournfully. 'I reckon it'll be raining before morning, Sister Wood,' he said. 'And there will be a few showers before then, I reckon.'

Alison laughed. Fred was always pessimistic about the weather.

'Don't say that, Fred. You'll spoil my day,' Alison replied as she turned away and began walking briskly towards the surgical block where she worked as senior theatre sister. As she walked, she hummed a catchy tune to the rhythm of her long, slender legs, deliberately

5

avoiding the joins in the flag-stoned path like a child on its way to school. Alison felt a strong sense of anticipation that something special was about to happen to her today. Something out of the ordinary. Not that she had any reason to expect anything, but it just seemed to be that kind of day.

As she rounded a turn in the path, Alison suddenly saw a black BMW sweep through the main gate and head towards the doctors' car park. Her heart skipped a beat as the sight of the big black car transported her back through time. Greg's car, she thought, stopping in her tracks and following the passage of the saloon with wistful eyes. Then, realising that she was being fanciful, Alison shook her head to clear away the unwelcome thoughts that were racing through her mind and laughed at herself.

Greg was still in America, where he had been for the last two years. That was all finished now, all over, kaput. She pulled a long face. At least the break had been clean, with no loose ends to complicate things and cause her further heartache. Why was it, then, that every time she saw that particular make of car her heart stood still and the butterflies started fluttering in her stomach?

Another car came through the gate. A red Alfa Romeo with Tom Saunders leaning out of the window waving to her. Alison's eyes crinkled into a smile as he mouthed the words, 'I love you,' before roaring away towards the car park. Tom was the senior registrar in Cy Harris's firm, a brilliant plastic surgeon who was already marked as a rising star. Tom was the hospital rake, devilishly handsome and with a line that had lured many an unsuspecting nurse off the straight and narrow path. He had been pursuing Alison ever since he had arrived at the hospital, but she, afraid of his reputation and with a heart still bruised from her affair with Greg, kept Tom strictly at arm's length.

Not that she found him unattractive. Quite the opposite. Once, in an unguarded moment, when she allowed him to kiss her during an accidental encounter in the lift, Alison had found the experience far from unpleasant, although always after that she made a point of never being left alone with Tom.

She turned into the pathway that led to the surgical block and instantly there came a chorus of wolf-whistles from some workmen who were on the roof of the new heart unit that was nearing completion. Alison quickened her step in an effort to escape them, but it was hopeless. The heart unit was a long, single storey building, and she would have to endure their gibes as she did every morning. But they were good-hearted men who meant no offence, and despite herself Alison had to smile at some of their remarks.

'Like to take my pulse, Nurse?'

'How about a bed bath, Nurse? It's my birthday!'

Alison stopped and looked up at them, a pink flush on her face.

'When do you think you'll be finished?' she asked, curious to know. The new heart unit was the talk of the hospital. It was to be a show-piece, rivalling similar units that had been set up in America, and although no appointments had been made there was intense speculation about who would run it on the medical side.

'Floor layers are coming in today,' one of the men called to her. 'And we'll be gone by the end of the week.'

Alison thanked him for the information and congratulated them on the handsome appearance of the building before hurrying on. She wondered who would get the medical appointment. Rumour had it that it was to be a man from America, one of the world's leading heart surgeons, and Alison found herself wondering what he would be like. Would he be as easy to work with as Cy Harris, her own boss? If so, she would be tempted to apply for a position in the new unit, for that would represent a fresh challenge to her skill and competence which she wouldn't be able to resist. There was one position, senior to the one she held at present, that was just made for her. She had all the qualifications and only her youth might count against her.

Alison entered the surgical block and called good morning to the young man on duty at the desk. He grinned and appraised her slender figure appreciatively before replying. Alison smiled back. She was used to men's admiring glances, although she made a point of not encouraging them. A tall, slender blonde, with a good figure, she was well aware that men found her attractive. She also knew that in their imaginations they assumed that a girl with her looks had dozens of suitors and a date every night.

Alison gave a wry smile and reflected on the life she actually led, divided between the arduous work of a senior theatre sister and caring for her sick mother. The fact was, she couldn't even remember the last time she had been on a date or even when any man had asked her out, except for Tom, who asked her every day.

She hurried to the notice board to read the day's theatre list. Thankfully it was short, and Alison read through the names with interest.

Most of the operations were routine; but one, the last of the morning, captured her interest. The name was

Carla Swain, daughter of millionaire financier Sir Maxwell Swain, the man who had endowed the new heart unit. Alison had been present when Cy Harris had first examined Carla, a lively fifteen-year-old, whose life was marred by a badly disfigured lip. The disfigurement had been made even worse by a previous operation which had been badly bungled and today's operation was to be a last, almost despairing, chance to put things right.

Alison was well aware that Cy Harris had only taken the case after much heart-searching, for the chance of complete success was extremely remote. Scar tissue from the previous operation considerably reduced the chances of restoring the lip and it must have taken enormous courage on Cy's part to have agreed to operate at all. Alison turned from the notice board with a sigh and made her way to her office.

She was too professional not to realise the danger of getting involved with a case, but Carla tore at her heart-strings. The girl was so brave it almost made Alison cry, but no one on earth could ever imagine what was going on in the poor child's mind; the suffering she endured in private.

When Alison entered her office her friend Mary Webb was already there. She looked up as Alison entered, a teapot in her hand.

'Cup of tea?' she asked, raising her eyebrows.

Alison nodded and laughed as she removed her light raincoat. Mary always started the day with a cup of tea. Sometimes Alison found it welcome, especially when she had had to leave home in a hurry and missed breakfast.

'Make it quick,' she replied. 'I want to go down to the ward to have a chat with Carla. She probably needs some reassurance on her big day and if I hurry I'll catch her before she has her pre-med.'

Mary shook her head disapprovingly. 'You get too involved, Alison,' she said. 'Honestly, you'll tear yourself apart one day.'

Alison laughed. 'I'm sorry, Mary,' she replied, 'but I can't help myself sometimes. It's the way I'm made, I suppose. I wish I did have your detachment, but I haven't. And even you have to agree that this is a rather special case, what with Sir Maxwell being so closely involved with the hospital. Just imagine what must be going through the poor child's mind at this moment. And she always seems so brave. I can't imagine facing life with a disfigurement like that.'

Mary smiled. 'All right, Florence Nightingale,' she responded. 'I have sleepless nights too! I'm not nearly as hard-hearted as I seem to be. Sometimes I wonder why I do this job.'

'You do it because you love it, Mary. Admit it, you wouldn't be happy doing anything else. I've never known such a caring person as you. You seem to love the whole human race.'

Mary pulled a face to cover her embarrassment. 'Perhaps you are right,' she said. 'But sometimes I wish it were different.' She paused reflectively and then laughed. 'I wouldn't mind someone tall dark and handsome caring for me,' she said. 'But you had better run along. I've had quite enough philosophising for one day and I have work to do.'

Alison stopped at the ward office for a word with the sister. On their way to Carla's room the other sister said, 'I'm glad you came, I've been worried about Carla. She has been very down-hearted and now she doesn't really

believe that anything can be done to help her. I hope
Mr Harris hasn't raised her hopes in vain because if
this doesn't work out I think she might break down
completely.'

Alison nodded her understanding, her spirits suddenly saddened by Sister's confirmation that Carla's
brave front had begun to crumble. She forced herself to
smile as she was shown into a side-room filled with
banked masses of flowers. A small table was crowded
with cards from well-wishers.

Carla, dressed in a very new-looking, floral-patterned
silk dressing-gown, was sitting with her back to the door,
looking out of the window. When Alison entered she
turned, her hand flying up instinctively to cover her
mouth.

'Hallo, Carla,' Alison said. 'I'm Alison Wood. I
thought you might be glad of some company for a few
minutes. I'm impressed by all these flowers. Why, you
could easily open a flower shop! You must have a lot of
friends.'

Carla nodded self-consciously and looked at Alison
with wide, questioning eyes. Alison noticed that her left
hand never came away from the region of her mouth and
her heart went out to the girl.

Carla was small and dark, with a trim, athletic figure,
but the most noticeable thing about her was her eyes.
They looked haunted, and Alison felt that she was
looking into deep pools of sadness. She almost cried at
the realisation that without her deformed lip, Carla
would have been an outstandingly beautiful girl.

'Mummy and Daddy sent most of the flowers,' Carla
said, her voice muffled by the hand that never left her
mouth. 'Because it's my operation today they came in to

see me early. Mr Harris came as well—he's only just gone. He had another doctor with him, a famous heart surgeon from America, terribly handsome, but he didn't sound at all like an American. He was nice. I liked him, and he said he would come back to give me my pre-med.'

Alison smiled. 'He seems to have made a big impression,' she said. 'He was really dishy, was he? What was his name?'

'Mr Verney,' Carla said animatedly. 'But he said that I could call him Greg.'

Alison's heart pounded and the hand that she extended to Carla was visibly shaking. 'Greg Verney?' she said weakly, her voice sounding little more than a croak. 'Are you sure, Carla?'

Carla nodded, her eyes fixed intently on Alison's face. 'Oh, yes,' she replied. 'It was definitely Greg Verney. Why, do you know him?'

Alison gave a wan smile, her heart pounding like a steam-hammer.

'Yes,' she confessed. 'I do know Greg Verney. As a matter of fact he used to work in this hospital a long time ago, before he went to America. But I had no idea that he had returned to England.' She paused, groping for the right words. Then, 'I don't suppose you know why he came? I mean, was it a social visit, or do you think Greg has business in the hospital?'

Alison awaited Carla's answer with bated breath. She knew that she shouldn't pump Carla for information, but she just had to know.

Carla glanced up suddenly with an awareness that caused Alison's cheeks to flare. Alison realised that Carla was not only intelligent, but she had the quick intuition of a girl just blossoming into womanhood. She suspected that more than idle curiosity had prompted Alison's question and she smiled knowingly before replying.

'He spent a long time talking to Daddy about the new heart unit,' she said. 'And he did mention that he might be looking for a house in this area.' Carla paused, looked sideways at Alison and with a smile on her face said, 'Nurse Soames told me that he had had an unhappy love affair and that was why he left England to work in America. Is that true?'

Alison managed a faint smile. She remembered Nurse Soames, who was one of the worst gossips in Parkleigh. She had a nose for any kind of scandal, particularly of a romantic kind, and spread it around the hospital like wildfire. At this moment Alison would willingly have wrung Nurse Soames' neck, for by now her old association with Greg would be all round the hospital.

'It sounds rather fanciful to me,' she replied to Carla's question. 'But if he did, I expect that's all over and done with by now. Don't you?'

Carla nodded thoughtfully. 'Imagine a girl turning down a man like him,' she said in an awestruck voice. 'I know I wouldn't . . .'

Carla's voice trailed away and Alison looked at her to see tears running down her cheeks. The pain in Carla's eyes was transparently obvious and Alison's heart went out to the unfortunate girl. She leaned forward and put a comforting arm around Carla.

'Carla, don't be frightened,' she said, holding the girl's dark head to her breast and stroking her hair. 'Everything will be all right, you'll see. Mr Harris has performed this operation hundreds of times. You couldn't wish for a more experienced surgeon.

And I shall be there with you.'

'I'm . . . I'm not afraid. Not of dying. I often wish that I *was* dead,' Carla sobbed. She turned her face to Alison. 'Wouldn't you, if you looked like me?' Alison saw again the appalling extent of Carla's disfigurement, the sight made even worse by the livid scar tissue left by the previous operation.

'Do you think that any boy would look at me with a face like mine?' Carla asked, desperation in her voice.

Alison choked back the tears that were threatening to flow. 'Oh, Carla,' she said, 'it isn't how people look on the outside that matters. It's what is in their hearts that counts. Believe me, Mr Harris is a brilliant surgeon. Trust him, Carla. In a few hours all the pain and unhappiness will be behind you and the whole of your life will lie before you.'

Alison gulped. She was well aware that she was behaving in a very unprofessional way and was glad that there were no witnesses to the scene.

Carla's tears continued undiminished. 'Mr Harris can't perform miracles,' she cried, 'and that is what I need. A miracle.'

Alison didn't know what to say. She had seen Cy Harris perform many miracles of plastic surgery, but now she groped for the words which would give Carla the reassurance that she so desperately needed.

'Someone in trouble? Can I help?'

Alison's back stiffened. The rich, incisive voice was unmistakable. She felt her body tremble as she turned to face the man who stood in the doorway.

She drew in her breath sharply as her blue eyes met the rich brown of Greg Verney's. He had scarcely changed at all. The lock of dark hair still fell boyishly

over his forehead as it always had, and his smile, lopsided as ever, still reached out and plucked at her
heart-strings.

Greg walked forward. If he had noticed Alison's
confusion, he chose to ignore it. 'Hallo Alison,' he said.
'It's been a long time.'

All Alison could think of was to get away as quickly as
possible, but her legs felt weak and she sat there,
transfixed by the almost hypnotic effect of his eyes. At
last, when she recovered her composure, she replied,
'I'm fine, Greg, but Carla is a little upset. Do you think
that you could find the ward sister? I think it's time for
her pre-med.'

Greg smiled at Carla and bent his six foot frame to
stoop down beside her. 'What has a gorgeous girl like
you got to cry about on a lovely day like this?' he said.
Then he produced a snowy white handkerchief from his
pocket and handed it to the girl. 'Here, dry your eyes. I
came back especially to talk with you, Carla. Tell me all
about it.'

Carla dried her tears and turned her face to Greg's
with none of the embarrassment that she had shown
earlier to Alison. There was complete adoration written
in her eyes that made Alison smile with relief. The tiny
crisis was over. Greg has found another slave for life, she
thought. Poor Carla, she doesn't know that loving Greg
is like a life sentence without remission.

Greg looked up. 'It will be quite all right to leave Carla
with me,' he said. 'But I will call in and see you later on,
if that's all right with you.'

Alison looked at her watch. It was time to prepare for
surgery. 'Thanks, Greg,' she said. 'I'll look forward to
seeing you later.'

She was still in a fluster as she changed into her green theatre garb. After her encounter with Greg Verney she seemed to be all fingers and thumbs and had difficulty in tucking her hair away under the new, disposable paper headgear. She smiled at herself in the mirror. What a sight she looked in the new dungarees that fastened tightly at ankles and wrists. Especially imported by the American company that owned the major shareholding in Parkleigh Hospital, they were made of the same material as the cap and took some getting used to, but Admin insisted that they saved a fortune in laundry bills and staff would have to persevere with them.

Alison walked into the theatre, wondering how her recent encounter with Greg Verney would affect her performance that morning. If Tom Saunders was operating she would need all her wits about her, for he worked at an incredible pace. But she needn't have worried. Once inside the familiar atmosphere of the theatre, all other thoughts left her mind and she set about her duties with an icy competence.

Cy Harris completed the first operation in just over half an hour. Fortunately, what was thought at first to be a serious condition turned out to be comparatively easy, requiring only minor surgery, and Cy conserved his energy by allowing Tom Saunders to complete the final stages of the operation.

The second case, the remodelling of a broken jaw, had been deferred to a later date, and Alison's heart skipped a beat as she saw Carla being wheeled into the theatre, her slight frame swathed in sterile robes.

After the initial incisions, Cy Harris used incredibly small instruments and viewed his work through a low-powered microscope that swung over the patient on a gantry attached to the side of the operating table. Only he and Tom Saunders could follow the progress of the operation.

Alison was aware of a growing inner tension as they worked in a silence that was punctuated only by the click of the shining steel instruments as she returned them to the tray.

At last, after nearly two hours at the table, Cy Harris straightened his back and swung the microscope aside. Now there was an almost tangible tension in the theatre as the intricate surgery neared its climax. Cy turned, and Alison noticed the signs of the almost unbearable strain showing in his eyes. He straightened his back and then inclined his head towards one of the junior nurses, who immediately stepped forward and wiped the thin film of perspiration from his forehead.

Alison's pulse began to race. Usually the surgeons chatted amicably while they were operating, but today there had been only silence and she knew that they were working at the limits of human skill. Suddenly the operation assumed an almost life and death importance, and not for the first time in her life Alison found herself praying. It had to come out right, it just had to. But with complete professionalism she succeeded in maintaining her outward appearance of complete calm. No one, watching her, could have suspected that behind her façade of ice-cool precision her mind churned with inexpressible fears.

Cy Harris turned to her, as he often did when he needed an extra hand.

'Hold this suture, please, Alison,' he murmured in a low voice. 'No, not with those tongs, use the small forceps. I need more space to work in . . . Yes, that's fine.'

Alison concentrated on maintaining a firm hold on the forceps while Cy Harris and Tom Saunders made an assessment of their progress.

Carla's inert body looked impossibly frail and Alison's eyes were filled with compassion for the girl. She was so defenceless against the cruel blow that fate had struck her, and her only hope for the future resided in the strong, sensitive hands of Cy Harris. Alison was aware that there was no finer person in his field than Cy. Each time she saw him work it was as if a miracle took place on the operating table, and she felt privileged to stand beside him.

At last Cy murmured that he was satisfied, and Alison released the suture before standing back, away from the table. Then, to her complete surprise, Cy turned to her and said, 'I think we'll give her a kissable mouth like yours, Sister Wood. After all, Carla is a very pretty girl.'

Alison was thankful that her mask hid the blush that she felt burning on her cheeks. From behind her she heard Angela Barnes, a very junior nurse, giggle on hearing the remark, and she smiled. Angela would have plenty to giggle about when she heard about Alison and Greg Verney on the hospital grape-vine.

Cy Harris began the last, critical stage of the operation. This was the moment of truth and everything depended on it, not only for Carla, but for the hospital as well. For according to the changing-room gossip, Sir Maxwell Swain had promised to completely equip the new heart unit, in addition to the endowments that he had already made, if the operation was a success.

Alison held her breath as she watched Cy's deft fingers tie the mass of sutures that would eventually be used to draw the reformed lip into place. The new unit was very dear to Cy Harris. He had spent almost five years in getting it off the ground. Unless Sir Maxwell provided the money it could take another five years to equip it to the standard which Cy had set his heart on.

Now he nodded to Tom, signifying that he was ready to continue, and Alison offered up a silent prayer. It just had to be right. It meant too much, to too many people, for anything to go wrong.

She held her breath as together the two surgeons manipulated the delicate network of sutures, each as fine as a spider's web. Then, slowly but surely, under the control of their sensitive fingers, a perfect Cupid's bow formed as if by magic. Alison glanced quickly at Cy and saw a smile flicker in the corner of his eye. At that moment her strict professionalism momentarily deserted her and a tear formed and trickled slowly down her face under her mask. Only she and Tom heard Cy murmur softly, 'Thank you, Lord.'

He stood staring down at his work, turning his head this way and that as he did so. Then he grunted his approval and turned to Tom Saunders. 'Will you stitch up, Tom? I think we've done quite a good job.'

Tom grinned and winked at Alison. Cy's comment was the highest praise that he ever permitted himself and it meant that the operation was completely successful. Alison could have cried with relief, and as Tom commenced stitching her heart sang. Within a few weeks, all that would remain to show that the operation had ever taken place would be a faint line, easily hidden by light make-up. And in months nothing would show at all. Carla would be able to lead the normal life of any lively teenage girl.

'By the way, Tom,' Cy remarked while the other surgeon completed his work. 'I would appreciate it if you will lunch with me today. I want you to meet Greg Verney. With any luck we can get him to agree to take over the new heart unit. He has already expressed some interest in the project, and now that I can tell him that the money is as good as assured I think it's time to persuade the Board to make the appointment of head of surgery and medical director. It's a combined office and will be quite a feather in our cap if we can get Greg to accept it.'

Tom Saunders paused, his brow furrowed in thought. 'I think he wrote a recent article about double valve replacement in the *Lancet*,' he said. 'If that's the Verney you mean it will be a privilege to meet him. But do you think there is a serious chance of getting a man of his stature?'

'Why not? He has a free hand to run things his own way. Completely new buildings and equipment as well. I think that's a pretty good deal for a man of thirty-two. There's another thing in his favour too. His family come from around these parts. You may remember that his father was a member of the hospital board until his death last year when Lady Verney took his place.'

Tom Saunders could be seen to grin at that, even under his mask. 'One of *those* Verneys,' he remarked. 'That's interesting. I somehow find it hard to connect a humble surgeon with that snooty crowd. Will I have to bow when I meet him, or will kissing his feet be enough?'

Cy laughed. 'It sounds as if you've already met Lady Verney,' he said. 'I agree that she is a bit much to take. But don't worry, Greg has his feet firmly on the ground.'

Alison listened with her mind in a whirl. She trembled in spite of the warm atmosphere of the theatre, and as she supervised the instrument count she began to feel increasingly faint. Then, to her dismay, Tom Saunders noticed her discomfiture and asked her if she felt well enough to continue.

With an effort of will she pulled herself together, her strict training quickly asserting itself.

'I'm fine, Tom,' she answered breathlessly. 'But it's rather hot in here this morning. I'll be all right in a minute.'

Tom nodded. 'It *is* rather hot in here,' he agreed. 'I noticed it myself.'

Alison was relieved when her explanation was accepted without further question and was glad when, with a quick smile in her direction, Tom left the theatre in the company of Cy Harris. As they passed through the door she heard him say, 'It was rather hot in the theatre, Cy. I think I shall get Maintenance to check the thermostat.'

Ten minutes later, her work for the morning over, Alison removed her theatre clothing and threw it into the disposal chute. Then she stepped under the shower and as the refreshing water streamed over her body her thoughts turned to Greg Verney. Memories that Alison had hoped were long forgotten came flooding back to her. It seemed inevitable, now, that she and Greg would be thrown together again. Would she be able to stand the emotional strain of that daily pressure? Alison smiled as she towelled herself. The brief encounter of the morning had given her the answer to that particular question. And it was a resounding, emphatic, *No!*

Soon, clad in her uniform dress of pale blue, with snowy collar and cuffs, she made her way back to the office which she shared with Mary Webb. She and Mary had passed through nursing training together and they had always been close friends. Although Mary had chosen to work abroad for a while, both of them were delighted when they found themselves together again at Parkleigh.

Alison was disappointed to find the office empty, for she had been keen to discuss the new development with Mary. To pass time she filled up the old teapot they used to water their pot plants, added a drop of liquid fertiliser and turned her attention to the greenery on the window sill.

Her mind went instinctively back to thoughts of Greg. If he really returned to the hospital for good it was going to turn her whole life upside down, that was certain. Of course, a lot might depend on his attitude to her. If he considered their past affair to be over and done with, that was one thing. Things might just about work out, even though Alison would have to give up her ambition of working in the heart unit. But if he wanted to take it up again where they had left off, that was quite a different matter. Alison had been hurt too badly to rush back into the arms of a man who had ruthlessly discarded her because she didn't match up to his mother's high standard of requirement for a wife for her precious son, and who thought her a cheat.

Alison's hand trembled and some water spilled on to the sill. As she fetched a cloth from the sink to mop it up with she laughed at herself. 'Stop reacting like a love-struck schoolgirl,' she said aloud. 'And all over a man who walked out of your life two years ago. What a fool you are, Alison!'

She put the teapot in the sink before there were any more accidents and turned to the morning's mail. Then, finding that her heart wasn't in reading through endless circulars from surgical supply houses, she tossed them into the pending tray, deciding that they would keep until later.

She turned to the mirror on the wall and began to comb her fine, honey-coloured hair into the semblance of a style. Like all the theatre staff, Alison found that the air-conditioned atmosphere made it impossible to do anything at all with her hair. She pulled it back tight with one hand and examined her reflection critically. Perhaps a short cut would suit her? It would certainly make it easier to manage. Alison pulled a face at herself in the mirror and combed her hair so that it curled around her neck. What she needed was the advice of a good hairdresser, she decided.

Just then Mary Webb entered the office like a whirlwind and threw herself into a chair.

'Phew!' she said. 'What a morning I've had in ENT—and there's more to come this afternoon. My feet are killing me.' She leaned back and put her feet up on the desk before turning her eyes on Alison.

'I say, have you heard the latest? Greg Verney is back in the hospital for good. The junior nurses are going crazy over him. Anyone would think he was Mick Jagger or David Bowie from the way they're carrying on.'

Alison smiled. 'I met him in the surgical ward,' she replied. 'And I don't think it's quite settled that he'll be returning to Parkleigh, though it is true that he has been offered the new heart unit.'

Mary looked at Alison in amazement. 'Gosh, I am sorry,' she said. 'Just like me to put my foot in it. I'd forgotten about you and him. You were having quite a ding-dong just before he left, weren't you? I hope it isn't still a painful subject.'

Alison shook her head. 'Not really, Mary,' she lied. 'After all, it was a long time ago. I don't mind admitting that it came as quite a shock, seeing him so unexpectedly after all this time. I thought he'd left England for good. Greener pastures and all that.'

She walked over to the window and stood looking out over the green fields that surrounded the hospital. Even the mention of Greg's name caused her face to burn and she didn't want Mary to suspect that she was nursing anything as dramatic as a broken heart.

Mary broke the silence first. 'Greg hurt you badly when he left so suddenly, didn't he, Alison?' she said quietly.

Alison nodded. It was no use trying to keep secrets from her friend, she realised. 'I might have known that it would end like that,' she said. 'A girl like me getting mixed up with the Verneys. It was obvious enough that his family were against him seeing me, especially Lady Verney. She really had it in for me.' Alison pressed her lips together and then gave a tiny laugh.

'Don't worry, Mary,' she said, seeing an anxious look steal over her friend's face. 'It won't happen again. From now on my heart is my own. I don't think I could ever trust another man with my life.'

Alison looked steadily into her friend's eyes and saw that she didn't believe her. And Mary was right, Greg Verney still had the power to send her weak at the knees. The truth was that Alison was still hopelessly, impossibly, in love with him—and from now on the even tenor of her life was to be interrupted by crises like that of this morning when she had inadvertently met him in the surgical ward.

'Things will soon settle down,' Mary said philosophically. 'I remember that we were all a little in love with Greg in those days. Not surprising really, considering how good-looking he is. There will be plenty of hearts beating faster in the nurses' home if he comes back to work here.'

Alison turned away from the window and began to put on her raincoat. She didn't want to talk about Greg any more. No one, not even Mary, would ever understand just how she felt.

'I must fly,' she said. 'I have to catch the shops on my way home.'

Mary nodded. 'Give my love to your mother,' she called as Alison left the office.

Absorbed in her thoughts, Alison took a short cut through the main entrance and was half-way across the doctors' car park when she noticed Cy Harris, Tom Saunders and Greg standing beside Cy's big grey Rolls Royce. They were deep in conversation and, hoping that they wouldn't notice her, Alison turned to go back into the hospital, intending to leave by another door. She had no wish to encounter Greg again—not until she had adjusted to the idea of his continued presence in the hospital.

But Cy spotted her and called out, and then both Tom and Greg turned to face in her direction, a smile of greeting on each of their faces. Flustered at being unable to escape, Alison approached them with her heart in her mouth. This was exactly the kind of meeting that she had been hoping to avoid. She was bound to do or say something foolish.

'Come and meet an old friend,' Cy said when she drew near to them.

'We did meet, earlier in the surgical ward,' Alison replied. 'But hallo again, Greg. How are you?'

Greg smiled, the same lopsided smile that always had

the power to melt her heart.

'Hallo,' he said. 'We didn't have time to talk much, we had a little crisis on our hands with Carla,' he explained to Cy. 'I'm glad to see that you are looking well, Alison. Cy has been singing your praises to me. In fact he just offered you to me as an inducement to take over the new heart unit.'

Alison looked at him, a bewildered expression on her face. 'I'm sorry,' she said, a faint smile coming to her eyes to cover the embarrassing thought that had sprung into her mind. 'I don't think we're on the same wavelength.'

Cy intervened. 'I've been telling Greg how invaluable you are,' he said, 'and I've as good as promised that if he takes over the new unit he could have you to take over the nursing side for him. If you are willing to, that is.'

'Me!' Alison looked at the three men in dumb amazement. She was as good as being offered the job that had been her dream ever since the foundations of the heart unit had been laid. But then she had not known that Greg Verney would be leading the surgical team. She swallowed hard, realising that to accept was impossible for her.

'It's a serious offer,' Greg said firmly, evidently well aware of the doubts that were racing through Alison's mind. 'And it's a plum job, carrying with it the rank of full Head of Nursing. You can't afford to turn it down, Alison.'

'But . . . Why me?'

'Because you are the best person for the job. Your record speaks for itself. Gold medallist at Guy's, the youngest nurse ever to attain the rank of sister in this hospital; why, Cy tells me that you've been running the theatre single-handed as well as organising the training schedule for new nurses. You are exactly the kind of person we need. Dedicated, hard-working and quick to learn. This is a big new field, Alison, and advances are being made every day. This could be the most exciting challenge of your life.'

Alison gulped, her mouth too dry to speak. If she took the job she would be working day after day at Greg's side. Could she ever learn to stand the emotional strain of being constantly in the company of the man whose wife she had once expected to be?

Greg was watching her face intently and his face was deadly serious. 'We aren't playing games Alison,' he continued. 'This is a vital project and I shall be needing the help of the very best people I can recruit if it is to be a success. And I don't intend to fail.'

Alison found her voice. 'But I have no experience of cardiac surgery,' she objected. 'It is a very specialised field.'

'I think you have every qualification that I require,' Greg replied quickly. 'Complete dedication and the ability to learn new skills. And if you decide to come in I shall arrange for you to be retrained in all the basic procedures.'

Alison's quick brain sought desperately for a means of escape, but it was obvious that Greg was in no mood to accept a blank refusal from her.

She raised her hand to her face in a gesture of self-doubt.

'This is rather too much to take in all at once, Greg,' she replied. 'I will need time to think it over.'

To her dismay he immediately began to press her. 'Look, Alison,' he said reasonably enough, 'you must realise that this job was made for you. Cy has been telling me how difficult things are at home with your mother being ill, but that problem can be resolved. Take a few days to think it over, by all means, but I think you will agree in the end that there is only one course that you can take. This is a really exciting project. If you can join us for lunch, I'll explain the plans that I have for it.'

Alison glanced at Tom, who was standing looking from Greg to her with an astonished look on his face. She remembered that Tom had no knowledge of what had passed between her and Greg and suddenly she wanted to laugh as she thought of what he would say when he found out.

She shook her head. 'I can't come to lunch, Greg. Mother is expecting me and I have some shopping to do. I really must be on my way, but I promise that I shall consider this offer very carefully.'

Then Cy, knowing about Alison and Greg's former relationship, and sensing that things were moving too fast for her, intervened.

'Sorry, Alison,' he said, glaring at Greg. 'We are all so caught up in our new toy that we can't think of anything else. You run along now, but don't forget to think this over very carefully before you come to a decision. But if you want the job, it's yours.'

'I'll be in touch very soon,' Greg promised as Alison turned to go. 'And remember, I don't intend to take no for an answer.'

As Alison walked to her car her mind was in a whirl. She remembered jokingly thinking that today was special, but nothing could have prepared her for this shock. Could she really handle a job as big as this? And in the company of Greg Verney?

CHAPTER TWO

THE COTTAGE in which Alison lived with her mother lay just on the outskirts of the small market town of Parkleigh. Alison had spent her childhood in the neat cottage and, except for the time when she had been away training in London and the period when she had worked in a big city hospital in the Midlands, she had lived there all her life.

Parkleigh was one of the bigger private hospitals, and Alison had taken the job there for the reason that it was conveniently near to her home, enabling her to look after her sick mother, who was suffering from a chronic heart disease. Alison didn't mind working in private medicine, unlike some of the nurses she had known who considered it wrong for people to be able to buy privilege of any kind. To Alison, sick people needed treatment whoever they were. But she had been surprised to find that the majority of patients at Parkleigh, far from being rich, were quite ordinary people whose employers contributed to medical insurance schemes on their behalf.

Alison loved the country life; walking along country lanes in the rain, or riding high over the downs on her horse, Snowball. From her bedroom window she enjoyed a glorious view out over rolling farmland, dotted here and there with ancient copses.

She arrived home to find her mother hovering anxiously near the front door. She smiled and waved as she walked up the garden path, appraising her mother's face for the tell-tale signs of breathlessness or the faint blueing of the lips which would indicate that she was having one of her bad days. Then, seeing nothing amiss, Alison kissed her mother fondly and hugged her.

'You're very late today, dear. I was beginning to get quite worried,' her mother said.

Alison smiled. 'Don't be such a fuss-pot, Mummy,' she replied. 'I know that you worry when I'm out in the car, even though you know perfectly well that I'm a very careful driver. I had some shopping to do, that's all, and I was held up at the hospital. I'll tell you all about that over lunch. Oh, but there is one piece of good news that won't wait. Cy operated on Carla Swain this morning and it went perfectly. She'll be as pretty as a picture. Cy is like a dog with two tails because Sir Maxwell is going to put up the money to equip the new heart unit. You know how much that means to him.'

Alison noticed how much the news pleased her mother, especially the news about Carla, but she couldn't help laughing when her mother said, 'Now dear. What's for lunch? I'll come and help you prepare it.'

Being almost entirely housebound, as she was, Alison's mother tended to measure each day by meal times, and they had assumed a tremendous importance for her. Patients in hospital were the same, especially in Parkleigh where they selected their meals from a wide menu.

'I'm afraid it's only salad today, Mummy. I haven't much time left and this afternoon will be rather a rush as it is.'

Over a hastily prepared meal, Alison told her mother all about her morning's encounter with Greg, and how he had offered her a position in the new heart unit now that he was definitely returning to Parkleigh. As she spoke, Alison noticed a curious look come into her mother's eyes every time she mentioned Greg's name and, guessing the direction in which her mother's thoughts were moving, she stood up abruptly and began to clear the table. The last thing she wanted at that moment was to have to answer awkward questions, and her mother had a habit of being brutally frank at times.

'There's just time for a cup of tea, if I'm quick,' she said. 'Would you like a cup?'

'Yes, dear.' Her mother looked at Alison thoughtfully as she filled the kettle. 'I always liked Greg,' she said. 'It will be nice for his mother to have him home again. The poor woman must live a very lonely life, now that her husband is gone.'

Alison looked up quickly. Greg's father had died suddenly a year ago. Then she smiled at the thought of Lady Verney being referred to as 'the poor woman' when the Verneys owned half the county.

'Yes, I suppose it will,' she replied. She stood up and gulped down her tea. 'Well, I'd better run,' she said. 'I'm lecturing this afternoon.'

As she drove along the narrow lanes, Alison thought about the contrasting lives led by Greg's mother and her own. Lady Verney was a total snob, coming, as she did, from an old county family who owned most of the land around Parkleigh. Lady Verney had never tried to disguise the fact that she considered Alison unsuitable for Greg and had even gone so far as to suggest to Alison that Greg was simply amusing himself with her until a suitable girl, from what she called 'a good family', came along. Moreover, she was a picture of health, while

Alison's mother had made herself ill with the strain of bringing up her daughter after her husband's death.

Alison sighed as she parked her Mini. The direction that her thoughts had taken had depressed her, in spite of the fact that it was still a glorious day. The irony of the situation was that when the new heart unit was completed and running, her mother might be saved. A new advance had been made in the hospital in Dallas where Greg had been working, but there was no way that Alison could afford the money to send her mother there, and time was running out.

Alison cleared her mind of her dark thoughts and began to prepare herself for the lecture that she was about to deliver to the junior nurses. Although, as a private hospital, Parkleigh had no teaching faculty, they still maintained a continuous training programme for the younger nurses, to keep them up to date with the newest advances. Alison enjoyed lecturing and had always played a full part in the teaching duties that were expected of her, unlike some of the other sisters, who avoided lecturing by making excuses about the pressure of work.

Alison found the class already seated in the lecture theatre, and from the sudden hush that descended as she took her place on the rostrum, guessed they had been discussing her.

There was some giggling, and then Angela Barnes, more daring than the rest, stood up and asked, 'Sister Wood, is it true that the dishy surgeon who was with Mr Harris this morning is coming to work here?'

There arose a loud chorus of 'oohs' from the rest of the girls, and Angela looked around the room with a smirk on her face, as if to say, 'There, I did it.' Alison guessed that Angela had been dared to ask the question and couldn't prevent a smile from crossing her face. Angela, with her blonde curls and wide blue eyes, reminded Alison of herself at that age, and because of this she had a soft spot for her, even though at times Angela was inclined to be a little impertinent. In time, she would make an excellent nurse.

Putting on as stern an expression as she could manage under the circumstances, Alison rapped sharply on the rostrum with her pointer. 'The dishy man, as Angela so charmingly put it, is Mr Verney, an eminent heart surgeon from America. And that is all I can tell you about him, so you will just have to wait until there is an official announcement.'

The girls immediately began chattering between themselves, causing Alison to bring them to order by rapping with her pointer again. Then, unbending, she added, 'I may as well tell you that the way to impress eminent surgeons is not by altering the hospital uniform to something which you consider to be more fashionable, Angela. It's by dressing neatly and tidily and by running an orderly hospital. Some of you have quite a way to go in that direction, I might add.'

The girls groaned in unison and then Angela, apparently undaunted by Alison's reference to her uniform, stood up and pressed on with her questioning.

'Someone said that you already know Mr Verney, Sister Wood,' she said. 'What's he like, I mean *really* like.' She rolled her eyes expressively before sitting down to a general roar of laughter.

Alison looked across the sea of smiling faces and blushed to the roots of her hair. 'Perhaps it is time we got on with our work,' she said. 'Please turn to page forty-three of your lecture notes. This afternoon's subject is hygiene in the operating theatre. Now Angela, what are the main ways in which infection can be transmitted?'

Even as she said the words, Alison realised that she was going to get very little sense out of the girls on this particular afternoon. It was obvious that Nurse Soames had spread the news about she and Greg already, probably during the lunch-break. The staff restaurant had always been a favourite gossip-shop among the nurses. The news was evidently something of a nine day wonder, but with any luck it would soon pass.

As Angela gave a carefully worded and accurate answer to her question, Alison looked over the shining faces that were regarding her with something like awe. The ice maiden, as Alison knew they referred to her behind her back, had been shown to have a human side, and the nurses were obviously delighted.

Alison gave the rest of her lecture automatically, avoiding the girls' enquiring eyes and feeling like a specimen under the microscope. It was with considerable relief that she allowed them to go five minutes before the allotted time. With a chorus of giggles and a hubbub of voices, they streamed out of the theatre, some of them glancing knowingly in Alison's direction.

Alison watched the last of them leave and then pensively collected her lecture notes together. This had been a small taste of things to come, and heaven alone knew what it would be like when Greg actually started work in the hospital.

With a heart-felt sigh, she rose to her feet and walked over to the window. It looked out on to a broad meadow in which a herd of black and white Friesian cows were grazing contentedly. Am I becoming like those cows? Alison asked herself. Grazing contentedly in my own little field while the rest of the world passes me by. Maybe she did need the stimulus of a fresh challenge, which the job in the new heart unit would provide. Alison knew that she would have welcomed it if only it didn't involve working day after day in close proximity to Greg Verney. Even the thought of such close contact turned her knees to jelly, and from past experience Alison knew that Greg was not a man who could easily be ignored. Far from it. He was the sort of man who dominated everything and everybody by the sheer force of his personality. When Greg walked into a crowded room, everyone noticed.

'Good afternoon, Alison. May I come in?'

Alison's back stiffened as, for the second time that day, she heard the rich, unmistakably deep tones of Greg's voice. She hesitated and then swivelled round on her heel to face him.

Greg was standing by the doorway, smiling at her with his head inclined on one side. 'Well, may I?' he asked again.

Alison moistened her dry lips. 'Yes, of course, Greg,' she said, regarding him uncertainly. 'What brings you back to the hospital?'

He smiled again and crossed the room with a few strides of his long legs. 'You do,' he replied. 'I want to speak with you. Alone.'

Alison looked up at him, her clear blue eyes sweeping over his well-remembered face as it all came back to her—her memories as fresh as if the intervening years had never existed. His dark beard was beginning to grow through, and there were fine laughter lines around his eyes that hadn't been there when he had left her two years ago. Greg had always been good-looking in a clean-cut, classical way, but added maturity had transformed him into an impossibly handsome man. It was little wonder that the younger nurses found his looks so devastating.

'If you want to ask me about the job,' she said, 'I can't give you an answer because I haven't decided what to do.' Alison's courage almost deserted her, but with an effort of will she continued speaking, her mouth dry. 'It's so difficult, Greg. I mean . . . knowing you before. Already it is all round the hospital that you and I were, well . . . close. Don't you think it will be impossible to establish a normal working relationship under the circumstances?'

Greg's eyes narrowed dangerously. 'No I don't,' he replied. 'And as for our relationship, I would have said that it went a great deal deeper than close. I know that it did for me. After all, we were on the verge of becoming engaged to be married.'

Alison felt the colour rising to her cheeks. 'But you never quite got round to asking me, did you, Greg? Instead you preferred to believe the lies your mother told you about me and went away to America, leaving me high and dry.'

Alison shivered inwardly, remembering that day as if it was yesterday. And remembering, too, the pitying glances of her friends and the sniggers of the not so friendly; trying to pass it off as if it meant nothing to her that the man she adored no longer wanted her, and deceiving no one. She turned her blue eyes up to Greg's face, no longer afraid; nothing could ever hurt her that much again.

'Why don't you admit that I just wasn't considered good enough for the Verneys, Greg?'

Outwardly, Alison's face held an expression of defiance, but inwardly her stomach churned with emotion. Already she regretted the words she had just spoken. For two years she had rehearsed this first meeting with him in her mind, and it had been nothing like this. In her dreams they had slowly rediscovered their love and she had melted into his arms while he told her gently that everything was going to be all right. Now she couldn't even remember a single word of the speech she had so carefully rehearsed and she knew that even if she could, there was no way that her voice would allow her to utter so much as a single syllable.

Greg's eyes held not a flicker of emotion as he looked down at her.

'I won't waste words in attempting to convince you that it wasn't like that,' he replied quietly. 'But I didn't come to see you to discuss the past.' He hesitated and looked questioningly into Alison's face as if expecting to find something written there.

Without waiting for him to continue, Alison said bitterly, 'It's no good any more, Greg. I'm not the stupid girl who used to worship the ground you walk on. I've changed.'

Greg rubbed his cheek with his hand. 'I'm sorry,' he said, shaking his head. 'This isn't what I intended. We shouldn't be quarrelling, you and I. There are no words that change the past. I came to speak about the future, Alison. We can build something together. That empty shell of a building can be a place of hope for thousands of people and we can do it. Why not forget what has passed and say you'll join me? As for the past, I'm content to let sleeping dogs lie if that's what you want. I knew it was all over when you didn't answer my letters.'

In the silence that followed, Alison could hear her own heart beating and prayed that Greg wouldn't notice the pulsing that she could feel in her neck. Greg had written to her for over a year after he left, but she hadn't replied to his letters; she didn't even read them. Instead, she had burned each one as it arrived. Even now she could see the blue flame and the paper charring and curling as it burned. At the time it had seemed a good way to get even with him for leaving her, but now she saw that it had been stupid and childish. If only she had read them! Looking into his eyes now, Alison realised that all her happiness had been written on the flimsy paper and she had destroyed it with her own hands.

She turned away from him and stood looking out of the window. The cows stood huddled in the shelter of the hedge and spots of rain were already streaking the window pane. She smiled. The whole world seemed to be crying. At least Fred would have the satisfaction of being right about the weather.

She turned back to Greg, who was standing regarding her with his deep brown eyes like fathomless pools. If only she could see what was going on in his mind. She noticed that his silk tie was slightly awry and smiled. It was just like him. He bought the most expensive clothes that money could buy and treated them as if they were rags.

Greg could have taken the easy path and stepped straight into the family business had he so chosen, but with a complete disregard for material possessions he had dedicated his life to medicine. Alison remembered the days when she had worked beside him in the operating theatre. That was Greg's world and he moved easily in it, his brown skin glistening under the powerful lights and the dark hair escaping from under his theatre cap. If Alison took the job that was offered she would return to that world, but with the difference that she was no longer Greg's girl, only another cog in the machinery of the theatre.

Breaking her chain of thought, he spoke again. 'I came to ask you to have dinner with me this evening,' he said. 'You and I have a lot to do, and the sooner we get things started the better. I want the heart unit operational within six months from now, and that will take every waking hour between now and then, especially for you because you will be responsible for recruiting the nursing staff.'

Alison shook her head. 'But, Greg, I haven't agreed to take the job!'

Greg smiled. 'I know that you will,' he said. 'Whatever you say, we were always a damn good team, and I don't intend to take no for an answer.' He leaned forward and placed both his hands on Alison's shoulders, looking deep into her eyes. 'What are you afraid of?' he asked. 'This is a great adventure, and I want you to be a part of it.'

His excitement in the project seemed to flow through his strong, surgeon's hands and convey itself to Alison. She desperately wanted to tell him that she was as excited about the heart unit as he was, that she wasn't afraid that she didn't have the ability to handle the job, only of working by his side for years to come, nursing an impossible love for him. Even, perhaps, attending his wedding to some social butterfly without a brain in her head, but with the right family background. Alison felt that she could never stand that.

He bent his head lower so that their faces almost

touched and for a moment Alison thought that he was about to kiss her. 'Well?' he asked gently.

'Ahem!' The cough sounded through the empty lecture room like a gunshot, and Alison wheeled round to see Angela Barnes standing in the doorway, a wide smile on her face.

'What is it, Angela?'

'I left my notes behind, Sister.'

Alison gave a nod to signify that Angela could collect her notes and turned nervously towards the window, smoothing her dress with trembling hands. Then, when Angela had gone, she turned to Greg.

'You're destroying my reputation,' she said, pulling a face and laughing. 'It won't be long before it's all round the hospital that we were seen alone together, suitably embroidered of course. Angela has a marvellous imagination.' She walked to the rostrum and picked up her notes. 'I shall have to go,' she said. 'I have work to do, and I want to get away before six tonight.'

'You have a date?'

Alison shook her head.

'Then I'll pick you up at eight. All right?'

'I don't think that would be a good thing at all, Greg. I need time to think this out, free from outside pressure, and you are assuming too much.'

'Eight o'clock,' Greg said. 'I won't be late.' He looked at his watch. 'I have to see some of the governors now. I had hoped to tell them that you were prepared to come in. Can I?'

Alison couldn't help herself. 'You're impossible!' she said, laughing. 'Don't you ever take no for an answer?'

Greg shrugged. 'I did that once before,' he said, 'but

I'll never do it again. See you at eight.' He raised his hand and turned away.

Alison stood and watched his broad back as he passed through the door, almost filling the opening. He was on his way to tell the governors that he had recruited the key senior member of his nursing team, of that she was certain, and there was absolutely nothing she could do about it. Within days Greg would have taken over the whole of her professional life and ridden roughshod over every objection of hers—but her private life was her own, and Alison intended to keep it that way.

The bleeper went in her top pocket and she walked quickly to the nearest phone and lifted the receiver.

'John Bateman here,' said an agitated voice. 'We need your theatre in a hurry, Alison. There's been an accident. A young motorcyclist has been pretty badly smashed up in the road outside the hospital and is bleeding internally. Every second counts I'm afraid, so don't hang around. By the way, it's going to be a pretty messy affair.'

The line went dead and Alison's mind flew to her days in casualty surgery when road accidents had been a daily occurrence. Although her theatre was primarily equipped for plastic surgery, she was pretty certain that she could find everything that they would need. The main difficulty was finding the nurses. Most of her own staff had never seen much blood and she knew better than to rely on them standing up to what was to come. She ticked off the nurses she knew could be counted on, Mary Webb for one, and by the time she reached the lift everything was clear in her mind.

She found John Bateman scrubbing up. 'Who is operating?' she asked, noticing that he was shaking visibly.

'I'll have to do it myself,' he said. 'There's no time to find anyone else. Reception are trying to get an anaesthetist for me, but if they don't find one soon I shall have to give an intravenous and hope for the best. He's failing fast.'

Alison's cool eyes swept over his white face. John's surgical experience was limited and it was brave of him even to suggest undertaking this operation. 'You start the anaesthetic, John,' she said. 'I'll find a surgeon.'

He looked surprised, but with obvious relief he entered the theatre where Mary Webb was attending to the young patient, whose injuries were horrific. It was a wonder that he could manage to cling to life at all.

Greg came as soon as he received Alison's phone call. While he scrubbed up, Alison described as well as she could the extent of the injuries, to which Greg listened attentively, obviously valuing her judgment. 'Ruptured spleen,' he commented, 'and God only knows what else we are going to find.'

They walked into the theatre together and Greg looked enquiringly at John Bateman, who shook his head. 'If his blood pressure falls much more I won't be able to hold him,' he said.

Greg worked fast, removing the spleen and tying off the torn arteries with a speed and precision that only Alison, of those present, had ever seen before.

She stood by his side, instruments and swabs passing from her to Greg and back again with clockwork precision. There was scarcely any need for words, for the almost uncanny rapport which she and Greg had always had was establishing itself at once.

At last John Bateman reported that the patient's

blood pressure had begun to rise again and Greg grunted his satisfaction.

'I'll stitch up here,' he said. 'And then we can set to work on that broken leg. At least he isn't going to die on us now. Is he breathing comfortably?'

John shook his head. 'I think we may have some broken ribs to add to our troubles,' he said.

Greg smiled. 'Never rains but it pours,' he said coolly. 'Can it wait or shall I do the leg first?'

John weighed up the situation. His admiration for Greg was obvious to see, and Alison knew that he had handled the anaesthetic like a veteran, considering the difficulty of the case. She had seen professional anaes- thetists lose patients who were not so badly injured as this boy was.

'I think you should see to the ribs,' John said. 'They aren't giving trouble at present, but the possibility is always there.' He looked at Greg for approval and was relieved to see the surgeon smiling encouragement to him.

'You're quite right,' he said. 'The point is that there is some blood in the pleural cavity which will have to be drained fairly soon. We don't want any further com- plications from that direction.' He turned to Alison. 'Could you ring the hospital at Marley and tell them that we have a patient for the intensive care unit?' he asked. 'He'll be ready to transfer in about two hours.'

Alison walked briskly to the phone. Intensive care facilities were lacking at Parkleigh but were part of the scheme of the new heart unit, in which they would play a vital part. Marley General Hospital served a wide area and had every modern facility, even though it was run on a very tight budget and possessed none of the luxury of

Parkleigh. Alison explained the nature of the emergency and was assured that a suitably equipped ambulance would be on its way directly. Then she returned to the theatre and took her place once more by Greg's side.

Another crisis had developed during her absence, and Greg was working feverishly, trying to stop the flow of bright arterial blood. It was everywhere, the floor underfoot was slippery and Greg's face and body were streaked bright scarlet. Alison guessed that a damaged artery had given way, and Greg had thrown caution to the wind and gone straight in, having no time to lose. Without the vital heart-lung machine the position was critical and Alison knew that the patient's chances at this moment were almost non-existent. But she knew, also, that while there was the faintest spark of life left, Greg would continue the struggle. It was not part of his nature to accept defeat.

Minutes passed before John Bateman told them that the patient's blood pressure had begun to rise again. Now they had time to breathe and Greg wiped his brow before changing his sterile gloves.

He closed the incision, tying one-handed surgeon's knots with all the ease of a conjuror, before stepping back from the table.

It was at that moment that Alison knew beyond any doubt that she would take the job in the heart unit, whatever it cost her.

Greg nodded to John Bateman. 'Thanks,' he said. 'You did a great job there.'

Alison smiled as John visibly swelled with pride, his lost confidence completely restored. Greg thanked the theatre staff and handed the patient over to John and Mary Webb before turning to Alison. 'We still work well together,' he murmured softly. 'Now, where do I clean up?'

Alison showed him into the surgeon's changing-room and returned to the theatre, where the nurses were already washing the instruments and stacking them into the sterilising drums ready for the technicians to collect. She had never seen the theatre in such a state before. The nearest it ever came to this was during nose re-shaping operations, the speciality of Tom Saunders, which were often very bloody affairs. She went into the office and rang Maintenance, instructing them to hose the theatre down and steam-clean the floor and walls. As she did so, Alison recalled the days when theatre clean-ing had been the responsibility of the nurses, watched over by a dragon of a staff sister. At Parkleigh the theatre walls were of smooth stainless steel, welded into place and with all the ancillary services piped in so that there were no crevices to harbour any source of infec-tion. They resembled something from the space age, and with them the possibility of cross-infection had, to all intents and purposes, disappeared.

Alison tidied a few things and locked the drug cup-boards, which were her personal responsibility, before returning to her private changing-room. There was something strange which didn't quite register in her tired brain, but with a shrug she peeled off her blood-stained paper boiler suit and stuffed it down the disposal chute before turning to the mirror and pinning up her hair in preparation for the shower.

The shower! In that instant she knew what had bothered her when she first walked into the room. The shower was running. Had one of the plumbers left it on? Alison recalled that there had been some trouble with the water supply in some of the showers.

'Is anyone there?' she called nervously.

At that moment the door opened and Greg stepped out wearing nothing but a towel draped around his middle. 'It's only me,' he said. 'I hope you don't mind, but the surgeon's shower seems to be giving trouble, either too hot or too cold. This one is just right now I've regulated it. I've left it running for you.'

'Greg, you shouldn't be here!' Suddenly conscious that she was wearing practically nothing, Alison snatched up a bath towel and held it in front of her. Greg was laughing at her and Alison couldn't help laughing too. 'Go away,' she said. 'Before you are through you will have torn my reputation to shreds. Supposing one of the nurses sees you coming out of here dressed like that?'

'Theatre nurses are used to the sight of male flesh, aren't they?' Greg commented. 'But I see your point. This won't do at all. What if it came to Matron's ears?'

Alison flushed at the thought and quickly bundled Greg out through the door into the corridor.

When he was gone she showered, aware all the while of the dangerous turn her thoughts had taken at the sight of his brown, athletic body, the hard muscle rippling beneath the satin-smooth skin. For the first time in two years the close proximity of a man had aroused in her an awareness of her own body, and she had enjoyed the sensation of her nerves tingling and her heart beating faster.

She had forgotten what an intensely physical man Greg was, and how even his brown eyes regarding her across a crowded room had seemed to reach out and touch her body, raising goose-pimples and sending delicious little shivers down her spine.

Just then, standing next to her with droplets of water glistening on his skin and smelling of her own delicately perfumed soap, she had desperately wanted him to take her into his arms; to feel once again the taste of his lips on hers. Had Greg felt that way too?

Alison shook her head as she rinsed away the creamy soap from her body. She knew Greg well enough to realise that he responded to the call of his senses. If he had wanted to renew their relationship he would have taken her despite any objections on her part. Not that she could have raised any; Alison knew her own nature too well to imagine that she could have resisted him easily, but resist him she must.

As she carefully towelled herself she reflected that it would be easy to control her feelings just so long as Greg continued to regard her in a strictly professional light. At least he hadn't shown any interest in her as a woman, and for that she must be thankful, being well aware of the bitter heartache that must inevitably ensue from any close relationship with him. Her past humiliation had proved that. He had probably found someone else, someone whom his family would welcome as a more suitable wife for a man of his standing in the tight little social group in which the Verneys moved. Perhaps he had met someone in America? In her mind's eye, Alison pictured a long-legged, brown-haired Texan girl with a full, generous mouth and white teeth. A stab of jealousy ran through her body at the thought of Greg in another woman's arms—something that she had not thought about for ages, although when Greg had first left it had haunted her all the time.

Alison was just finishing dressing when Mary Webb came into the room and flopped down in a chair. 'Gosh, what a day!' she said. 'Still, I think the boy is going to be all right. He is breathing well and his pulse is pretty strong, considering the amount of blood he lost. By the way, his parents are down in recpetion asking to speak to someone about him. I told them that you would be down shortly. You don't mind, do you? They're awfully worried. He's their only child, you see, and they blame themselves for letting him have the motor bike.'

Alison was standing removing the pins from her hair. 'I won't keep them waiting long,' she said. 'What's their name?'

'Johnson, they live in the council houses behind the recreation ground.' Mary paused. 'Lucky that Greg Verney was in the hospital,' she said. 'Otherwise this story might have had a very different ending. He worked miracles in there, didn't he?'

Alison removed the last pin and shook her head, causing her hair to fall in graceful curls around her neck.

'I'd forgotten what working with Greg was like,' she said. 'He's a marvellous surgeon, isn't he? And it was good of him to praise John Bateman. It made John's day.'

Mary looked at Alison's shining eyes with a half-smile on her face. 'Of course, it couldn't be that you are biased,' she remarked, a strong note of irony in her voice. 'It couldn't possibly be that those soulful brown eyes are working their old magic on you?' She laughed. 'Seriously,' she continued, 'how can you even consider turning down the chance of working with Greg again? Gosh, I know I wouldn't, not after some of my experiences with the sawbones who call themselves consultant surgeons. Working with Greg Verney is my idea of heaven.'

Alison picked up her purse and turned to go. 'But I am taking the job, Mary. I decided in there just now, or rather Greg decided for me. You're right, I'd be mad to turn it down.' She hesitated and then continued. 'It isn't absolutely final because there are one or two things to sort out yet, but if I do take it, will you come with me and be my number two? I shall need someone on whom I can rely absolutely, and I think there may be times when I shall need you to lean on.'

Mary beamed and sprang to her feet. 'Gosh, *would* I?' she said enthusiastically. 'Just try to stop me. When do we start?'

Alison smiled. Mary's enthusiasm was going to be a tremendous asset.

'Steady on!' she said. 'Don't knock me down!' She glanced down at her watch. 'I must fly, the Johnsons have been kept waiting long enough and Mummy will be like a cat on hot bricks, wondering what's become of me. We'll talk it over in the morning after I've seen Greg. What do you think? He's taking me to dinner tonight.'

Mary opened her eyes wide and hummed the first few bars of Mendelssohn's wedding march.

Alison shook her head. 'This is strictly business, Mary. I'm not going to make the mistake of getting involved with the Verneys again, thank you. I'm still nursing my bruises from the last encounter.'

The lift stopped with a click at the ground floor, and Alison stepped out into the reception area, her eyes picking out the Johnsons immediately. They were sitting nervously on the edge of their seats, looking very worried and obviously overawed by their surroundings.

Alison's heart went out to them as she walked briskly towards them, a gentle smile of encouragment on her face.

They hung on to Alison's every word as she first assured them that their son would survive and then briefly described the extent of his injuries and what had been done by way of treatment. Their eyes opened wide when Alison informed them that he was being transferred to the intensive care unit at Marley, but she quickly pointed out that this was only because Parkleigh had no facilities for treating accidents or emergencies and this seemed to satisfy them.

Alison arranged for a porter to take the Johnsons to the staff restaurant for a cup of tea and then went to the admin office to hand in the keys to the drug cupboards. Inside she was surprised to find Tom Saunders, who was sitting on the edge of the desk chatting to the pretty young secretary who was on duty that evening. Alison smiled. Sally Bent, the secretary, was new to the hospital, fresh from secretarial college, and it was common knowledge that Tom had been trying out his smooth line of chat on her.

Sally looked up, slightly pink-faced, as Alison walked into the room and put the keys down on the desk.

'Don't believe a word he says, Sally,' Alison told her. 'He's a terrible liar.' Then, turning to Tom, she asked, 'What brings you back to the hospital, Tom?'

He laughed and then said, 'I came in answer to the emergency call, believe it or not, but when I arrived they said that Greg Verney had things well in hand, so I hung around to see if I could help in any way. I suppose the flap is over now?'

Alison nodded. 'They are transferring the patient to

intensive care over at Marley. I'm just on my way home.'

Tom took her arm. 'I'll walk you to the car park,' he said. 'You can fill me in on what happened. We don't get much excitement at Parkleigh, do we?'

Alison laughed. 'Oh, I don't know,' she said. 'There is always you, Tom. I think that having you around is excitement enough.' She smiled and waved goodnight to Sally before leading the way to the door. Outside she said, 'I hope I didn't break anything up, walking in on you like that.'

Tom put his arm around her waist and squeezed her. 'If only you would say yes, I wouldn't have to look at anyone else. By the way, how about dinner tonight?'

They were just entering the reception area and Alison gently twisted out of Tom's encircling arm. 'Sorry, Tom. Tonight I'm spoken for. Some other time, maybe.'

As she spoke, Alison noticed a tall, dark-haired girl come in through the main doors and stand looking around her. Then, seeing Alison and Tom, she came straight over to them, her hips swaying gently as she walked on elegant high-heeled shoes. Alison heard Tom give a low whistle.

'Excuse me,' the girl said, 'can you tell me where I can find Greg Verney? I have an appointment to meet him here, but I've been waiting outside for ages and there is still no sign of him.'

Alison felt her stomach churn as she looked at the girl's perfectly oval face framed by dark hair. Her full lips were parted in a smile, revealing small white teeth like pearls. If this was Greg's girl, she was lovely. Far lovelier than Alison's imagination had conjured up while she had been showering. When Alison tried to speak, she found to her dismay that her mouth had gone completely dry and no words emerged.

Tom stepped into the breach. 'I'll have Greg paged,' he said. 'What name shall I say?'

The girl smiled. 'Marcia Dupont,' she replied.

Tom took the girl's arm and steered her towards the reception desk. 'I'm Tom Saunders,' he said, 'and this is Alison Wood, an old friend of Greg's. Have you known him long, Marcia?'

Marcia looked quizzically at Alison and then replied, 'We met in Dallas last year. My firm has an office there and I was sent over for a while.'

Tom nodded. 'You are quite old friends then,' he said, shooting a glance at Alison. 'Do you live in this district?'

Marcia laughed. 'Heavens, no!' she replied. 'I have a little flat in Chelsea. As a matter of fact I've never been to Parkleigh before, although I expect to spend quite a lot of time down here in the future.'

While they were waiting, Alison began to fidget. There was no way that she wanted to see Greg and Marcia together. She glanced at her watch.

'I'll have to run, Tom,' she said. And then, turning to Marcia, 'Goodbye. I hope Greg won't be too long.' Then she looked enquiringly at Tom, who was quite obviously willing to stay and talk to Marcia. It was little wonder. Marcia was so stunning to look at that Alison felt positively dowdy in her hospital clothes.

Marcia flashed a dazzling smile in Tom's direction. 'Don't stay on my account. I'm sure Greg won't be long now. It was awfully sweet of you to help me.'

Alison felt sick. It was quite obvious that Marcia could twist Tom around her little finger. She found herself wondering how Greg reacted to Marcia's dark beauty. As Tom walked her to her car after tearing himself away, he suddenly remarked, 'Greg Verney certainly seems to be a hit wherever he goes.'

Alison gave a brittle laugh. 'You sound quite jealous of Greg, Tom.'

He smiled. 'I shall be if he starts dating you, Alison. Marcia is a dish all right, but she wouldn't win a beauty contest if you were in the field. Not if I were one of the judges. As a matter of fact I find these ultra-sophisticated women rather off-putting.'

Alison laughed aloud at this. 'I certainly noticed how put off you were, Tom,' she said, her voice generously laced with sarcastic overtones. 'Well, I liked Marcia. She was lovely. Friendly, too. I think we could become friends on closer acquaintance.'

Tom raised his eyebrows. 'Is that so?' he replied enigmatically. 'I would have thought that you would be more likely to tear one another's eyes out. Or isn't it true about you and Greg Verney?'

Alison flushed. So it had reached Tom already. She stopped by her car and turned to face him.

'What are they saying, Tom?' she asked. Alison trusted Tom, she knew that he would tell her the truth, however unpalatable it was.

'Only that you and Greg were inseparable and that just when everyone thought that the pair of you were on the way to the altar he upped and left for America, leaving you pretty cut up about it. And that is why you never go on dates and sit with the older set at hospital dances, because you're still carrying a torch for him.'

Alison flinched inwardly. The story came very close to the truth and unless she took steps to dispel the idea that she was still in love with Greg she would become an object of pity again. She had no intention of becoming known as a hospital wife, like other nurses she had known, worshipping a doctor during the day and then going home to an empty room while he returned to a wife and family.

She looked at Tom earnestly. 'Tom, I know you fool around a lot, but underneath there is something, isn't there? I mean, we are friends, aren't we?'

'Of course we are,' Tom replied. He gave a sudden glance in Alison's direction, his eyes curious. 'If there is anything I can do, just ask,' he said. 'From what I've heard you are going to have a difficult time and I'll be glad to help you through it.'

Alison smiled. 'I think I'd like to take you up on those offers of dinner that you make me almost every day. I'm not promising a romance. In fact I can't promise anything except that I'll try to be good company. But you would be doing me a great favour. I think I've sat in during the evenings quite long enough and it's time for me to get out and about again before I become old before my time.'

A light smile hovered around Tom's lips. 'I've been thinking along the same lines myself,' he said. 'About you, I mean. It will be a joy to put some sparkle back into those lovely eyes of yours. But as for romance, we'll just have to wait and see, won't we? I certainly can't promise not to fall in love with you, Alison.'

Alison laughed. 'What! You, fall in love? I can't believe that a hardened campaigner like you would do anything so foolish, Tom.'

CHAPTER THREE

ALISON cooked her mother a light dinner and sat talking things over with her while she ate. She couldn't eat a thing after her encounter with Marcia, and in any case she still entertained a faint hope that Greg would keep their dinner date.

They discussed the new job and Alison couldn't help smiling as her mother pointed out how useful the extra money would be.

'After all, dear,' she said solemnly, almost causing Alison to burst out laughing, 'you do have to think of the future. I used to hope that you would marry Greg and settle down, but when that fell through you just sat indoors and never went anywhere. I don't know how you expect to meet any suitable young men when all you do is go out riding or walking on your own.' Her mother paused and Alison fought with herself to keep a straight face. 'Anyway,' her mother continued, 'if you really intend to be an old maid you will need a good income. You'll have this cottage, of course, but it takes money to keep it going.'

Alison leaned forward and covered her mother's hand with her own, looking at her with an intense feeling of tenderness in her heart.

'Mum, to hear you talk, anyone would think that I had one foot in the grave. I'm well qualified and good at my job, and I certainly don't intend to remain single. I have all the normal feelings, you know. I want a home and children, nappies on the line and grubby fingerprints on the paintwork. It's just that I was knocked sideways a bit, that's all. I felt that I could never trust a man again, but I feel different now. As a matter of fact, Tom Saunders has asked me out, and this time I'm going. How about that?'

Alison stood up and began to clear the table, leaving her mother watching a favourite television programme. It was after seven, and if Greg didn't ring to call off their date within the next ten minutes she would have to start getting ready.

The ten minutes passed while she was washing the dishes and Alison hesitated. It would be foolish to get ready only to be stood up, and there must be every possibility of that now Marcia had put in an appearance. As Greg's girl, Marcia would certainly have first claim on his time.

Alison walked slowly upstairs to her room, conscious that if Greg didn't turn up she would be very disappointed. She thought of Marcia and threw herself disconsolately full-length on the bed. Perhaps it would be just as well if Greg didn't come. She certainly didn't have anything in her wardrobe to match the beautifully designed boutique casuals that Marcia had been wearing. And definitely nothing suitable for the expensive restaurants that Greg frequented.

She rolled over and swung her long legs off the bed and crossed to her wardrobe. Apart from a few cotton frocks she had practically nothing suitable for any social occasion, let alone a dinner date. As she shuffled the dresses along the rail Alison began to hope that Greg wouldn't turn up—it would be too embarrassing. Surely she remembered having something dressier than these sorry-looking things? To Alison, at that moment all her clothes looked good for nothing but sending to the Scouts' jumble sale. She furrowed her brow. What had become of the blue silk dress that she had bought for the hospital dance? Surely she hadn't been foolish enough to give *that* away?

Downstairs she put her head into the sitting-room and called to her mother. 'Do you remember what happened to my blue silk dress, Mummy? I can't find it anywhere.'

Her mother thought for a while and then said, 'I think it's in the wardrobe in my room, dear. It's hung there for the past two years with a polythene cover over it.'

In a flash Alison remembered. She had put the dress in her mother's room because she didn't want to see it again. She had bought it to wear to the hospital dance just before she and Greg had split up, and he had never seen her in it. It was the most expensive dress that Alison had ever had and she had bought it especially for Greg. She rushed to her mother's room and took it down from the rail. Then, slipping off the polythene cover, she held it up to her body and examined herself in the mirror. There was no denying that the dress flattered her, and the heavy silk felt good as new. And it would still fit her, for if anything she had lost a pound or two during the past two years.

Crossing her fingers that Greg would turn up after all, Alison put on the barest minimum of make-up before dressing carefully. The heavy silk of the dress felt like heaven against her skin and she swung round in front of the mirror like a child, causing the skirt to swirl around her thighs. Then, from the lowest drawer of her dress-ing-table, she took out the white Italian lace stole that

Greg had given her one Christmas and, conscious that she had never looked lovelier, went downstairs to wait for him.

The doorbell rang as she put her foot on the bottom tread, and with her heart pounding and a feeling of trepidation, Alison glanced quickly at herself in the hall mirror. She looked radiant, but she was glad that her blusher hid the colour that her excitement had caused to rise to her cheeks.

Greg stepped hesitantly into the tiny hallway, almost filling it. In his hand he carried an enormous bouquet of deep red roses, their heavy scent quickly filling the room.

'You look gorgeous,' he said, looking at her thoughtfully. Then he held out the flowers. 'I brought these for your mother. Can I give them to her myself, or is she in bed?'

Suddenly feeling very small and shy, Alison looked up at him. 'Greg, they really are lovely!' she exclaimed. 'Mum is in the sitting-room watching television. Go through.'

Greg gave the flowers to her mother and stood chatting for a while before glancing at his heavy gold watch. 'We'll have to hurry,' he said. 'I booked a table at the Cartwheel for eight and it's past that now.'

Alison's mother beamed at them. 'Have a lovely evening, darling,' she said. 'And don't worry about me. I shall go to bed as soon as the play is over.'

As they left the cottage Alison felt Greg's hand on her arm. Remembering Marcia, she tried to pull away, but his grip was firm and masterful, as if he were taking her over. Alison set her lips in a firm line, saying nothing, but intending to make it quite clear to him that although she would be happy to work with him, that was where it ended. Alison didn't propose to play second string to Marcia Dupont.

When they were both seated in the car she said quietly, 'I want to make it quite clear, Greg, that as far as I am concerned this is strictly a business meeting.'

There was a short silence before Greg answered, and when he did his voice was all innocence. 'I don't understand,' he replied. 'Who suggested that it was anything else?'

Alison flushed. 'What became of Marcia?' she asked casually. She glanced at Greg and saw a slow smile spread over his face.

'You met Marcia?' he asked. 'Yes, it was awkward, her turning up like that. She wasn't due down here until tomorrow. Still, I managed to put her off. She's gone back to town.'

'I bet you didn't tell her that you were taking a girl out to dinner,' Alison said hotly. 'I think that's despicable after her coming all this way to see you. You could easily have phoned me and explained.'

'Do you really think so?' Greg's voice was quiet, but with a steely ring of menace in it. 'Well, that makes two of us. I think it was pretty despicable of you not to answer my letters, as a matter of fact. Tell me, why didn't you? I kept writing for over a year. Was it because there was someone else? Tom Saunders, perhaps.'

Alison shrugged. Although inwardly she felt far from composed, she didn't intend to let Greg see how his words affected her.

'There didn't seem any point in answering them. After all, you made it pretty clear on the night you left that things were never going to be quite the same again between us. Or do you think that it was all my fault that we split up?'

Greg snorted scornfully. 'I wouldn't have said that it amounted to much more than a misunderstanding. We could have sorted it out if I hadn't been forced to leave the next morning. In any case, I admitted that it was all my fault in my letters. You might at least have had the decency to reply to them.'

Alison's temper flared suddenly. 'Is that what it was? A misunderstanding?' she retorted. 'You said some cruel things that night, Greg. I was a vulnerable girl who worshipped the ground under your feet. I wanted desperately to believe that you didn't mean those things. But when it came to it your mother was too strong for me. She always made it quite clear that I wasn't good enough and in the end she made you believe it too. As for those wretched letters that you seem so concerned about, I didn't read them. If you must know, I burned them!'

Alison leaned back in her seat, her heart pounding, conscious that she had quite deliberately tried to provoke Greg and not knowing why she had done it or how she expected him to respond. Feeling like a naughty child who has overstepped the mark, she glanced nervously at him. It had been stupid of her to rake up the past when tonight was intended to be a kind of new beginning, even if it wasn't to be the kind of new beginning that her heart longed for.

Greg sat quietly, outwardly calm, although Alison noticed that his knuckles, as he gripped the steering wheel, were white with strain. Her stomach churned with inexpressible fears as she waited for some response from him.

At last he relaxed. 'You damned little fool,' he said. And then he laughed aloud—almost with relief, Alison thought.

And as the churning inside her slowly died away she wondered what had been in the letters that Greg was so glad to discover she hadn't read them. The impulse to ask him was on the tip of her tongue, but Alison thought better of it; the past had already driven between them like an irremovable wedge. It was better that she allow Greg to make the next move while she was in this mood.

He expertly negotiated the narrow lanes, driving fast but in perfect safety round the winding bends. Alison looked around the car, which was obviously new, though the same make as his old one. Greg must have bought it in the knowledge that he was intending to stay in England, and that could only mean that he had already made up his mind to head the new heart unit well before the meeting today. She smiled. Only Greg would be arrogant enough to decide on a course of action without even knowing the terms that he was to be offered, confident that he would get what he wanted.

He slowed down at the junction with the main road and Alison looked round in surprise as they passed an entrance to a farm, the gateway half-hidden by high, overgrown hedges.

'It's been sold!' she exclaimed. 'I wonder who bought it? I hope whoever the new owner is won't charge me too much rent for my field. Mr Wooster let me have it for nothing.'

The car lurched as Greg swung out of the lane and accelerated hard. 'What was that?' he asked.

'The old farm has been sold. While you were away it came up for sale. Mr Wooster's arthritis got so bad that he couldn't work it any more and he went to live with his sister in the village. They put the farm up for sale six months ago and I'm interested, now that it's sold, to find the new owner. The field behind our garden is part of the farm.'

Greg shrugged as he turned off the road into the car park of the Cartwheel and slid gently to a halt. 'Field rents don't amount to much, do they?' he asked. 'I dare say he will let you have it for a few pounds a week.'

'Well that's a lot to me. I suppose I could always find someone to share with, but that always seems to lead to trouble in the end. I used to share with some people who took my feed for their own horses.'

Greg laughed. 'Well, if you take the job, you won't have to worry about a few pounds a week. It carries a pretty substantial salary. You haven't thought any more about it, have you?'

Alison nodded. They were in the entrance lobby now. It was a pretty room with oak beams and sporting prints on the walls.

'I've decided to take it,' she said. 'If you can stand me, then I think I can stand you. I decided this afternoon. It was super working with you again. As you say, we make a good team. In the theatre, at any rate.'

Greg looked deep into her eyes, his own crinkling into a smile, and it was all Alison could do to prevent herself from hugging him.

'Welcome to the team,' he said. 'Do you realise that you are my first recruit? I think this calls for a celebration. What will you have?'

Alison considered for a moment and then looked up at Greg, an elfin smile on her face. 'Can I have a Jelly Bean?' she asked.

His face registered surprise. 'Sure. Anything at all. But what is it? Do you drink it or suck it?'

Alison giggled. 'I don't know,' she replied. 'I've never had one, but the junior nurses say they're lovely and I've been longing to try one.'

With a bemused expression on his face Greg ordered a Jelly Bean for Alison and a malt whisky for himself from the poker-faced barman.

'Looks good,' he said when the barman returned carrying a glass of cloudy pink liquid. 'I don't think I'll ask what's in it.'

Alison sipped at it tentatively. 'Mm,' she said, 'this is delicious. It tastes all fruity.'

Greg lifted his glass. 'Here's to the new heart unit,' he said. 'And to our success.'

Alison's face clouded as she remembered the operation that Greg had performed and the worried parents of the injured boy. 'I do hope that boy pulls through,' she said. 'Did you go to Marley with the ambulance?'

Greg shook his head. 'I had an appointment,' he replied. 'John Bateman and Sister Webb went with him. He was still holding his own when I phoned earlier, though. There's no reason why he shouldn't pull through; no brain damage.'

Alison nodded and thought with a pang that the appointment that Greg had mentioned had been with Marcia Dupont. She sipped her drink, her eyes flickering around the room, avoiding his. She had to stop thinking about Greg being with other women or life would become impossible. Only the work must count from now on. She thought what a fighter Greg had always been. That afternoon he had dragged the boy back from the brink by sheer determination and an almost miraculous surgical skill. He had always hated to lose a patient. Once someone had said that he had too much heart to be a surgeon, implying that he became too involved on a personal level. It was true, Alison knew, but it was also true that Greg's deep humanity drove him on, making him refuse to accept defeat.

Greg touched her nose gently and Alison looked up, smiling.

'What are you thinking about so earnestly?' he joked. 'You don't have to worry about that boy. He'll pull through.'

At that moment the restaurant manager arrived on the scene and Alison was relieved that she didn't have to invent an answer.

The man was new to the place and Alison noticed how obsequious he was to Greg. He couldn't have known him personally, but the Verney name was sufficient to obtain the very best that the restaurant could offer. Alison smiled inwardly as the man fawned over Greg. At any moment she expected him to lick his hand and Greg's discomfort was very evident from the way he carried himself.

'The price of fame,' Alison mocked as the manager walked away and directed a waiter to attend to them immediately.

Greg leaned back in his seat and looked over the table with a sick expression on his face.

'That man is insufferable,' he said. 'If this keeps on happening I shall find a quiet pub where no one knows me.'

The waiter placed a bowl of roses on the table and lit a single red candle, placing it slightly to one side so that they could have an uninterrupted view of one another.

Alison bent her head and pretended to be reading the menu. Greg was quite obviously becoming annoyed and she felt that at any moment she would burst out laughing.

'Have you decided what to order?' he asked, obviously on edge.

'Can I be a pig and have avocado followed by the roast duck?'

'Of course—but isn't that a rather fattening dinner? I thought all girls nowadays watched their waistlines.'

Alison shook her head. 'Not this girl,' she said. 'I can eat whatever I like without putting on weight. There was a girl with anorexia in one of the wards a few months ago and that was enough to put anyone off dieting.'

Greg ordered a rare steak for himself and then called for the wine list. 'Anything special you would like?' he asked.

Alison shook her head. 'I'll drink anything expensive,' she replied. 'If I'm going to be a rich man's plaything for an evening I might as well enjoy it.'

Greg looked up sharply. 'You talk as if you had plenty of admirers,' he said quickly. Then his face relaxed into a smile. 'Or is that an awkward question?'

Alison laughed, thinking of the quiet social life she had been leading. 'Oh, hundreds,' she replied.

Greg tore a piece from a bread roll and said casually, 'Anyone special?'

She laughed. 'What do you think, Greg? I work an eight—sometimes nine—hour day and on top of that I have a sick mother to take care of and a house to run. When would I get any time for socialising? Usually I'm ready to drop by ten.'

To her annoyance Greg smiled and she began to wish

that she hadn't been quite so truthful about her lack of a social life and had told him a few white lies. When he learns that I am seeing Tom Saunders it will take the self-satisfied smile off his face, she thought smugly. If Greg was going to flaunt Marcia then she would do the same, and Tom was no mean catch, she had to admit, in spite of his reputation where women were concerned.

'I thought that there might be something going on between you and Tom Saunders,' Greg remarked casually. 'I noticed the way he looked at you, and he was definitely trying to warn me off while we were lunching.' He looked thoughtfully at Alison across the table. 'Seeing you in that dress, I'm surprised that the guys aren't buzzing around you like bees after the honey.'

Alison smiled. Greg had picked up quite a few American mannerisms of speech during his stay in Texas, as well as a definite twang, which she found rather attractive.

'I shall have to tell Tom that warning you away from me just isn't necessary,' she said acidly. 'Not that I think you'll have any more trouble from Tom. He was with me when I met Marcia. Tom knows you're spoken for now.'

A puzzled frown passed over Greg's face, but it cleared as quickly as it had appeared. Alison thought for a moment that he was about to say something, but instead he turned to the wine waiter and ordered a very expensive Veuve-Cliquot champagne.

Then he leaned forward, his familiar, lopsided grin on his face, his eyes warm and embracing. 'You've rather taken the wind out of my sails,' he said. 'I had carefully prepared a number of compelling arguments to induce you to take the job, but now you've given in without my striking a blow. If it isn't an awkward question, what finally decided you? You were very lukewarm about the whole thing this morning.'

Alison straightened her back and shook her head, causing her hair to sway around her neck and throat. 'I suppose it suddenly struck me that it was too good an opportunity to miss,' she replied. 'And working with you in the theatre this afternoon really clinched it. As you said, we are a good team.'

Greg smiled. 'We may as well get down to business then. I want you to recruit two complete theatre teams of the best available nurses. I've drawn up a staffing list which I shall give you tomorrow, but the main thing is that we must have experienced nurses, preferably un-married. It takes quite a time to build up a group that can work together like clockwork and I don't want the whole thing upset by babies or complaining husbands. The other thing is that I've agreed not to poach staff from Parkleigh, so you will have to spread your net wide—outside the area altogether, if necessary.'

Alison immediately thought of Mary Webb. 'I must have Mary,' she said, a worried frown crossing her brow. 'I shall need a good number two to lead the other team and there is no one I would rather have than Mary. She's the girl who was in the theatre this afternoon. Well, you saw for yourself how good she is. We've worked together for years and we get on well. I must have her, Greg.'

Greg looked thoughtful. 'I can't promise anything, but I'll see if I can twist Cy Harris's arm in the morning. He's in the mood to give me anything I want right at the moment. She isn't thinking of getting married, is she?'

Alison laughed. 'You seem to be obsessed by mar-riage,' she said. 'Most women get married eventually, you know, and so do men. *You* aren't thinking of getting married, by any chance? You seem awfully interested in other peoples' plans in that direction.'

Greg was intent upon cutting his steak and without looking up he said, 'As a matter of fact, I am. If she'll have me that is.'

Alison felt her heart stop and then begin to thump unmercifully against her rib-cage. A vision of Marcia's cool beauty flooded her mind and she felt sick with suspense.

'Do I get a prize for guessing who it is?' she asked, bowing her head and toying with her food. Her mouth went totally dry and she drained a glass of champagne at a gulp.

Greg looked up and grinned at her. 'None at all,' he said. 'It's too easy.'

'Have you asked her yet?'

He shook his head. 'There are a few difficulties to iron out yet, but I'm quite confident that they can be disposed of. It's high time I settled down. Unmarried doctors always cause a few raised eyebrows.'

Alison felt that it was time to be magnanimous. After all, she had realised all along that she was clinging to a very faint hope where Greg was concerned. Now that Marcia had arrived on the scene it was better to put a brave face on things.

'I liked Marcia,' she said. 'I expect we shall be seeing quite a lot of her now.'

Greg smiled. 'I'm glad you like her,' he said. 'It will certainly make things easier. Later, when you know her better, you will find that she has some very exceptional talents.'

Alison wondered what Marcia's talents were. Something artistic, for certain. Everything about Marcia proclaimed that. And she must be successful in whatever it was to afford the clothes she had been wearing. She was too gregarious to be a writer or a painter, they were lonely occupations, and Alison couldn't imagine Marcia alone for long. A television studio or an advertising agency was probably nearer the mark.

'I'm surprised that you aren't thinking of settling down,' Greg said, suddenly breaking into her train of thought.

Alison pretended to laugh, although inwardly her stomach gave a lurch as a picture formed in her mind of Marcia in a white dress standing in the little village church where she and Greg would have been married.

'I sometimes think I already have settled down,' she replied. 'What with looking after Mummy and Snowball and housekeeping, I've become quite domesticated.'

Greg raised his eyebrows. 'I've been meaning to ask you about Snowball,' he said. 'You mentioned him in the car. I take it he is a horse?'

Alison smiled and nodded. 'I bought him just after you left. I do quite a lot of riding at weekends.'

Greg looked interested. 'I shall be buying a couple of horses,' he said. 'It's something I missed while I was away. Cy tells me they are starting the drag-hounds again. We shall have to ride out together.'

'Oh. What would Marcia think about that?'

'For a moment I had forgotten Marcia.' Greg leaned back in his chair. 'To be honest, it's difficult to remember anything with you sitting across the table from me in that dress. You really do look stunning this evening, quite out of this world.'

Alison shifted uneasily in her seat. This was getting

dangerous. Was Greg hoping that she would be a second string to his bow? If so it was a notion that she should very quickly dispel. But it was nice to be complimented by Greg again. Alison smiled across the table at him. He really was the most deliciously attractive man she had ever known; outwardly gentle, but with a hard centre and an iron will, when he chose to exercise it.

Stubborn too. Alison remembered the row when they had split up and how he had refused to back down, even when she had proved herself innocent of having an affair with a married consultant. It was an idea that Greg's mother had planted in his mind when she had seen Alison travelling to London in the consultant's Rolls. In reality all that she had been guilty of was accepting a lift, but she had stayed in London overnight and by the next day when she saw Greg the poison had worked deep into his mind, the more so because his mother had claimed that she had seen Alison and the consultant kissing in a lay-by. Alison wondered if Greg still believed that story or if it was no longer of any account now that he had met Marcia.

'Hey, you're very thoughtful this evening! I pay you a compliment and you don't even answer.'

Alison looked up to find Greg smiling at her. 'I'm sorry,' she said. 'I keep getting lost in my thoughts. It's very rude of me, I know. It was a lovely compliment. Thank you.'

Greg indicated a waiter, who was approaching with a trolley. 'Something from the trolley?'

Alison feasted her eyes on the array of fattening confections. 'Mm. I'll have some of that gateau, please. A double helping with cream.'

Greg gave her order to the waiter. 'You would be a

wow in Texas,' he remarked. 'All the women over there are on strict diets and are as thin as rakes. They mistakenly believe that it makes them appear younger than they are.'

Alison noticed that Greg's eyes were wandering appreciatively over her body and she flushed, conscious of the effect of the soft silk draped over her full breasts and wishing that she had not drawn attention to her figure by ordering a double helping of gateau. To distract Greg's attention she asked for some dessert wine.

Immediately, he ordered a glass of Sauternes for her. Alison adored Sauternes and the combination of the chilled, sweet wine with the light chocolate sponge and dark, bitter cherries was mouth-wateringly delicious. She savoured every spoonful down to the last crumb of chocolate.

Greg watched her eat with evident delight, choosing for himself some of the new Lymeswold cheese, which he had never tried before. 'Was it good?' he asked.

'Mm. But I feel an absolute pig!'

Greg laughed. 'Shall we have some fruit, or are you ready for coffee?'

'Coffee, please. I couldn't eat another thing.'

The lounge was a comfortable, elegantly panelled room, with oil paintings of hunting scenes around the walls, in keeping with the rural nature of the locality. They sat in huge armchairs while the waiter placed their coffee on an oak table together with two glasses of cognac. Alison felt warm inside and sleepy, as if she were about to nod off. All her nerves about being with Greg again had gone, and she was beginning to feel that coping with his return to Parkleigh might be easier than she had expected.

Greg moved his chair close to hers so that the arms were touching. 'We have to get down to some serious talking now,' he said.

Alison looked at him in surprise. 'I thought it was settled?'

Greg relaxed in his chair and stretched his long legs out in front of him. 'This is about something else,' he said. 'It concerns your mother and I want you to consider what I say very carefully.'

Alison nodded and leaned forward, cupping the huge bowl of her brandy glass in both hands.

'I went to see Dr Patel this afternoon,' Greg continued, his eyes studying Alison's face carefully.

Her heart missed a beat. Dr Patel was her mother's consultant cardiologist. 'Oh?' she said, wondering what was coming next.

'He showed me your mother's records and we discussed her case in some detail. Somewhat irregular, since I'm not officially on the staff yet, but I assumed that you wouldn't mind.'

Alison nodded, her heart thumping uncontrollably. Did Greg have bad news for her? Was he about to inform her that her mother was even worse than she feared? She placed her brandy glass down on the table, worried that it might slip from her grasp.

'I won't beat about the bush. Your mother's condition is extremely serious. The heart valves were severely damaged in the original attack of endocarditis and although the original infection cleared under antibiotics there has been a pronounced deterioration over the past six months. She needs an immediate operation to replace the valves—and possibly the wall of the right ventricle will need reinforcing too.' Greg shrugged and gave a half-smile. 'If the new unit was ready we could operate here, but until it is, I'm arranging to use surgical facilities in a private clinic in London. I want to put your mother at the head of my list.'

Alison listened in stunned silence, a sense of hopelessness engulfing her. Surely Greg must be aware that she could never afford the cost of such treatment? And her health insurance didn't cover this eventuality. 'But . . .' she began.

Greg interrupted her. 'I rang Jason Hunt—he is the top consultant in the John Hopgood clinic in Dallas—and he agrees that it would be dangerous to wait. He is willing to come over here to assist me when the time comes, but for the present I want to admit your mother to Parkleigh so that I can run some tests.'

Alison's elation was quickly replaced by a sense of cold reality. She shook her head. 'Greg, I can't possibly raise the money,' she objected. 'Even if I sell the cottage it wouldn't cover half the cost of the treatment.'

Greg leaned forward impulsively and took both her hands in his.

'We'll talk about the money when your mother is well again,' he said. 'But in the meantime, don't worry about it, I'll arrange everything.' His face creased into a smile that seemed to enfold her, protecting her from harm. 'At least there will be no surgeon's fees,' he said, 'and Jason Hunt will give his services free—he owes me a favour or two. And after the initial period in Intensive Care your mother can be transferred to Parkleigh to recuperate.'

Alison nodded. Staff and their families were entitled to free accommodation at Parkleigh. Suddenly everything that Greg had suggested seemed possible and her eyes filled with tears. She remembered the feeling she had experienced that morning; the strange sense that something special might happen. It had! Greg had come back into her life and turned her quietly ordered world upside down. She looked down at the fingers enclosing hers, the dark hairs curling from his wrist, and with a feeling almost of relief, realised that the future lay in Greg's hands now.

Alison blinked hard to hold back the tears that were scalding her eyelids and shook her head.

'Greg, I don't know what to say, or how to thank you,' she stammered. She smiled at him through the mist of tears that was beginning to cloud her blue eyes. 'But I think that I may be going to cry any minute now. Can we go?'

Greg released her hand. 'Good idea,' he said. 'How about driving over to Marley? We can reassure ourselves that the Johnson boy is comfortable before I take you home.'

He rose to his feet in one easy movement of his athletic frame and wrapped Alison's stole around her shoulders protectively. 'It's been quite a day, hasn't it?' he remarked as they walked from the lounge.

Alison nodded, noticing that their exit was being followed by curious eyes.

They found Mrs Johnson keeping an all-night vigil outside the intensive care unit at Marley hospital. Alison stayed and talked to her while Greg, accompanied by an overawed Sister, went in to see his patient. Mrs Johnson explained that her husband had to work the next day and that she had sent him home.

'I'll be happier here,' she said. 'And I should never be able to sleep in any case.' She looked at the closed door through which Greg had just passed. 'Was that the

surgeon who saved Tim's life?' she asked, and when
Alison answered that that was indeed the case she said,
'I overheard the doctors here say that he was a miracle-
worker—that no one else could have done anything for
Tim.'

Alison didn't know what to say. It was the truth. Very
few surgeons would have taken the risks that Greg had
when the weakened artery had given way. It was immensely reassuring to know that Greg was to operate on
her mother.

Just then he appeared at the door of the intensive care
unit accompanied by the sister-in-charge, who was dancing attendance on him with something like adoration in
her dark eyes.

Alison introduced Mrs Johnson, who clung to Greg's
hand, her face lined with the strain that she was under.
Greg smiled warmly down at her.

'You must go home and rest, Mrs Johnson. Tim will
be fine now. In six months he'll be as good as new.' He
took her arm. 'Come along, I'll run you home in my car.
You can't help Tim by sitting here all night making
yourself ill. Believe me, he'll be fine and looking forward
to seeing you in the morning.'

Alison followed them along the scrubbed corridors as
Greg spoke quietly and reassuringly to Mrs Johnson.
Marley Hospital had none of the luxury of Parkleigh,
which more resembled a six-star hotel than a hospital,
but she knew that the medical care provided was second
to none—superior in many ways to anything that Parkleigh could provide.

After they had dropped Mrs Johnson, Greg settled in
the driver's seat and indicated a rack of tapes under the
dashboard. 'How about some music to soothe away the

cares of the day?' he said. 'You choose.'

Alison found that they were all old favourites of Greg's; hers too, for they both shared the same taste in music. Each piece seemed to hold some special memory for her of some poignant moment spent with Greg. She selected a tape and slipped it into the player and the car became filled with the hauntingly lovely strains of the overture from *A Midsummer's Night's Dream*. Alison's mind flew back to a holiday that she and Greg had spent together in the Loire valley, motoring slowly from one chateau to another, suspended in time. She closed her eyes as she recalled how much in love they had been, and smiled to herself as she remembered long-forgotten incidents—like how Greg had sulked when she had insisted on single rooms, and how guilty she had felt to refuse him anything that he desired. He must have loved her very much in those days to have put up with her naive views on love and sex so patiently. And yet in the end he had believed her capable of having a sexual affair with a married man . . .

She opened her eyes and glanced covertly at his finely wrought classical profile. What a complicated mixture he is, Alison thought. The truth of the matter was that she had never really understood the fiercely possessive sexual nature of his love. The powerfully creative side of him that made him a surgeon, combined with the stubborn pride of all the generations of Verneys stretching back in time to the Norman conquest, had its destructive side, too. It was a bitter irony that only now, after she had lost him, did she fully understand him. Alison hoped that Marcia could give him the kind of love he needed. Sexual and spiritual mingling so that their minds and bodies were one. Alison reflected how cruel it was that life so seldom offered second chances. If ever she fell in love again she would hold nothing of herself back from the man she loved. She would give everything of herself, body and soul, without fear. Not that it was likely to happen, for Greg was her one and only love. If she had never quite known it before he returned, she knew it now—and he must never suspect it, or their whole working relationship would become clouded by the knowledge.

She unbuckled the seat-belt as the car slid gently to a halt outside her cottage, feeling a profound sense of disappointment that the evening had ended. Greg turned and looked quietly into her eyes as the music faded and they were left sitting in a silence broken only by the low hooting of a distant owl.

Suddenly he leaned over to her and brushed away the single tear that was rolling down her cheek with his lips.

'Sentimental,' he murmured softly. Then, before Alison was aware of his intentions, his lips brushed gently against hers. An electric thrill ran through her body and she started back, afraid.

'Greg, please. This isn't fair,' she cried, aware now of the fluttering of her own heart and an overpowering need to feel his body close to her own.

His soft, strangely gentle eyes seemed to hold her. 'Just a goodnight kiss,' he said. 'It's no big deal.'

'But *Marcia*,' she whispered before his lips sealed hers, cutting off further protest.

Afterwards, still conscious of the musky smell of his aftershave and the hard feel of his body through the fine material of his suit, Alison sat shaking while Greg regarded her quietly, holding her with his warm brown eyes.

'Thanks for a lovely evening,' he said quietly. 'I really did enjoy myself. Now don't forget to break the news to your mother as soon as possible. She will need time to get used to the idea of an operation and the sooner things get moving, the better it will be.' Greg touched the tip of her nose lightly with his finger and smiled reassuringly. 'Don't worry,' he said. 'Everything is going to be all right.'

Alison pulled a face and didn't answer. Everything except my poor heart, she thought to herself.

CHAPTER FOUR

'HEARD the latest?'

Alison looked up to see Mary Webb bearing down on her carrying a plate of gooey-looking cakes and a cup of coffee on a tray.

Alison smiled. 'You know I don't get the gossip now I'm over in the new unit with Greg. What's all the excitement?'

'Well, Angela Barnes was seconded to Marley for a week on contract.' Mary sat down and sank her teeth into a cream bun. 'Mm, these are gorgeous,' she said.

Alison looked enquiringly at her. 'There's nothing unusual about contracting nurses to other hospitals,' she said. 'Admin have built contract work up into quite a thriving business. It's good for the nurses too. They get the extra pay as well as useful experience in other hospitals.'

Mary rolled her eyes. 'Some experience!' she remarked. 'It seems that two young housemen took a fancy to Angela and it came to a fight. Now they are under a week's suspension and Angela has been politely returned to us under a cloud.'

Alison laughed. 'It always was on the cards that Angela's flirting with doctors would land her in trouble. There was a skirmish over that young madam at the Christmas dance last year, I remember.'

'I think it is the doctors who cause all the trouble,' Mary added quickly. 'The amount of attention some of these youngsters get, it's bound to go to their heads.'

'Mm.' Alison looked knowingly at Mary, remembering an incident in which two student doctors had been suspended for a term. And Mary certainly hadn't been blameless over that episode. She had played them off against one another quite shamelessly.

'I think we've all had our youthful follies,' Alison remarked. 'I think Angela will be a super nurse when once she settles down. She has everything going for her—a quick brain, a caring attitude to patients and a cheerful disposition.' Alison paused. Angela had always been a favourite with her; was it possible that she tended to gloss over her faults? 'Anyway,' she went on, 'how are you looking forward to coming over to Cardiology? You can only have a few days left in the theatre now.'

Mary pulled a face. 'Roll on next Tuesday,' she said. 'I can't get out fast enough now. Your replacement, Sister Lewis, is a real tartar and no mistake.'

Alison laughed. 'You needed someone hard to sort you all out,' she said. 'I was far too soft on you.'

'Maybe, but we got the work done and enjoyed doing it. Now Staff Nurse Carter is threatening to resign and go back into the Health Service and Sister Lewis is being an absolute bitch to Angela Barnes since she came back from Marley. There's a terrible atmosphere down there.'

'What has she got against Angela? I always found her very willing.'

'It's all because Tom Saunders flirts with Angela and not her. You won't be popular with her either when she finds out that Tom is dating you! Underneath that crabby exterior is a soft little heart and it's pining for Tom.'

Alison raised her eyebrows. 'Really? She doesn't look the sort. How does Tom take it? I suppose he has noticed.'

'He plays up to it like mad—you know how he enjoys female adulation. She brought him in a cake the other day, said she made it herself, but I think she bought it in Marley bakery.'

'Who is being catty now, Mary?'

'All right, I admit it, I am,' Mary said, laughing. 'But honestly, I can't stand her. Let's change the subject. How is your mother? It must be more than a week now since she was admitted for tests. Greg Verney doesn't waste much time, does he?'

Alison blinked. Was it only a week? Time seemed to have lost all meaning for her since the day Greg had returned to Parkleigh. It must be a month since she had sat with him in his car, feeling as if a whirlwind had struck her, and yet so much had happened that it seemed like only yesterday! She had forgotten what a human dynamo Greg was; always on the go. He seemed to be everywhere; ordering equipment, interviewing staff for the unit, attending clinics in London—and on top of all that he had insisted on personally supervising the tests on her mother, spending hours on the phone consulting with his friend Jason Hunt in Dallas about her condition.

'Mum is fine. Her tests are all satisfactory and it is just a matter of waiting for the big day. A bit nail-biting, but Greg says there is nothing to worry about. His friend is bringing over some heart valves from Dallas—apparently they have to be specially made. When they arrive it's all systems go. Mum is terribly excited about it. She wants to get back to the world of the living, poor dear, instead of sitting around at home unable to do much or go anywhere.'

Mary looked pleased. 'It's incredible what strides have been made,' she said. 'I never imagined, when I first specialised in theatre work, that I should be getting into open heart surgery. Actually it's a bit daunting to think about.'

'It isn't the surgery so much,' Alison replied. 'That really comes down to highly skilled cutting and stitching, Greg says. But the machinery and instrumentation are like something from outer-space. Still, in a few months we shall look on it as just part of the theatre furniture, which is all it is, really.'

'Let's hope so.' Mary pulled a face. 'Well, I must dash. Tom has one of those messy nose jobs on and you know how he likes everything set just so. Oh, and one piece of news that might interest you. Clea Daventry was admitted today, only don't say I told you because it is very hush-hush.'

Alison looked up in surprise. Clea Daventry was a well-known actress.

'Really! That will put Parkleigh on the map. What is she in for?'

'Face-lift, what else? And guess whose patient she is? Tom Saunders'. Quite a feather in his cap.'

'Good for Tom. Who put her on to him?'

'Lady Swain, of course. You remember Carla? Her Ladyship was so pleased with Tom's stitching up that she is recommending him to all her snobby friends. He'll be riding around in a Rolls before the year's out. If I were you I'd put a "keep off" notice around his neck! By the way, everyone is sworn to secrecy. Clea Daventry doesn't want the press to get on to it, for obvious reasons. They might start enquiring into her real age, I suppose.'

'What's she like? As a person, I mean?' Alison was intrigued. Celebrities were scarce at Parkleigh.

'Gorgeous, actually. Makes me want to spit, considering she must be fifty if she's a day. And terribly friendly to the nurses. I mean she is a really nice person. Just goes to show, doesn't it? Well, I really must run now, see you.'

Alison smiled at her empty coffee cup. Five minutes with Mary and she had caught up on most of the hospital gossip. She glanced at the clock on the wall and rose to her feet. She had to see a batch of interviewees at half-past eleven and it was twenty-past already. At least there was no longer any talk about her and Greg as there had been when he had first arrived back at Parkleigh. Tom's attentions had effectively squashed that speculation, causing not much more than a few raised eyebrows. Tom's fleeting affairs were usually regarded with nothing more than an amused shrug, not worth discussing.

At the entrance to the cardiology unit Alison found Greg standing supervising a group of workmen, who were unloading a large flat stone from the back of a lorry.

'Hallo, what's that?' she asked.

'Hallo Alison. It's our commemorative stone. Sir Maxwell has been so generous to us that I thought it would be a nice gesture if we put up a stone with his name on it. Later on we'll have an unveiling ceremony and a party to celebrate. Give everyone involved a chance to let their hair down.'

'Good idea. Send me an invitation, won't you? Sorry I

can't stay, I have another batch of interviews and I'm late already.'

'Sure—oh, and by the way, I shall be going up to London for the rest of the day so you will have to hold the fort. Some people from an electronics firm are coming in to install the patient monitoring system in the intensive care unit. Keep an eye on them, will you?'

'OK. I'll come back from lunch early.' Alison smiled and looked at Greg's tired face. He was taking too much work on and it was beginning to show. On top of the new unit, Greg had taken on the post of consultant cardiologist at Marley hospital and was attending patients in a private clinic in London where he was going to operate on her mother. Alison was beginning to become really concerned about him and often wondered why Marcia didn't insist that he ease up.

Alison sat down at her desk and flicked open the file containing the curricula vitae of the candidates. They were all very impressive, as she had ascertained on the previous evening when she gone through them all in detail.

She looked up as there came a light knock on her door and the first girl was shown in by a junior from the personnel office.

The interviews passed smoothly. Personnel had done their screening well and the short-listed girls were all excellently qualified. Alison's only real concern was to ensure that they would fit into a team. Nevertheless, by the time it was all over, she felt drained of energy. She glanced at her watch to find that it was already ten minutes to two. The technicians would be arriving to install the equipment in the intensive care unit at any moment.

Alison tidied the files and put them away before

putting the kettle on. If she hurried there was time for a cup of coffee before she went along to the intensive care unit.

The kettle was on the point of boiling when Tom's head appeared round the corner of the door. 'Hi, beautiful,' he said, walking into the room. 'I smell coffee. Allow me to join you.'

Alison smiled and neatly avoided his arms, but she offered her cheek to be kissed. 'Hallo, Tom. It will have to be quick—I'm due in Intensive Care. Some people are coming to install the monitoring equipment.' She carefully spooned instant coffee granules into two cups and added hot water. 'Milk and sugar?' Tom nodded, his eyes never leaving her face. 'I hear I have to congratulate you on landing a prestige face-lift,' Alison said. 'Mary Webb told me about it earlier.'

Tom clicked his tongue in annoyance with himself. 'Sorry, I meant to tell you myself,' he said. 'But it all happened in a rush. One minute it was all in the air and then the next it was on. One word in the wrong place and I wouldn't have got it. You've no idea how touchy these actresses are about their public image. She is booked in as Mary Smith—how about that?'

'Mary said she was rather sweet. How do you find her?'

'I'd like her better if she didn't behave as if she were twenty years younger than she really is. Every time I look in on her she starts flirting with me quite openly. I ask you!'

Alison laughed aloud on seeing Tom's outraged expression. Clea Daventry was well known for keeping company with a succession of young men, most of them far younger than Tom.

'I would have said you were too old for her, Tom, but it's poetic justice in a way. Now you know how these young nurses feel when you chase them!'

'Ha, ha, very funny,' Tom said, sitting down at Alison's desk. 'I wonder who you could possibly mean. Not Sally Bent, by any chance?'

'Could be, Tom, except that Sally is a secretary. A little bird told me that she was in the Swan the other evening with John Bateman. Don't tell me you've let her slip through your fingers?'

Tom grinned. 'Can't win them all,' he said. 'Anyway, I'm losing interest in the hunt.' He looked enquiringly in Alison's direction before picking up his coffee cup. 'How about dinner this evening?' he asked. 'We haven't had an outing all week.'

Alison yawned. 'I don't know, Tom. I've been looking forward to an early night. Some other time, maybe. How about Saturday? Then I can lie in on Sunday morning.'

'OK, it's a date. But how about inviting me round to listen to records this evening if I promise to leave early?'

'You really are impossible, Tom.' Alison smiled and looked at him. It was very difficult to refuse Tom anything, she found. 'Oh, all right. But you will have to promise to leave before eleven. I shall drop if I don't get some sleep.'

Tom raised an eyebrow. 'Greg working you too hard?'

'There have been quite a few late nights recently. The trouble is that he seems to start around six after everyone else has gone and work through until midnight. You don't know how glad I shall be to get back to theatre work again! This endless paper-pushing drives me mad. Every single detail has to be double-checked.'

'You should have stayed with plastic surgery and

hob-nobbed with the stars of stage and screen, my girl. By the way, I saw the plaque on the wall as I came in. When is the opening ceremony?'

'It hasn't been decided yet. The plaque was Greg's idea to thank Sir Maxwell for his generosity to the hospital. Which reminds me, how did Carla's operation turn out? Mary was singing your praises, so it must have been pretty successful.'

'It was, even though I say it myself. If I belonged to the Women's Institute I should enter it for the needlework competition. Carla's lip would win the pot of home-made chutney easily.'

Alison laughed. 'There is no need to be irreverent about the Women's Institute,' she remarked. 'Mummy belongs, or did, before she was taken ill. But I'm glad it turned out well for Carla. Poor little thing, she must have suffered terribly, especially after that first operation went wrong.'

Tom smiled. 'And the moral of that is, always deal with a reputable firm if you want a good job. Trusty Tom always delivers the goods. I think I'll have a plate made with that engraved on it.'

'Don't you ever take anything seriously, Tom? In any case, I seem to remember Cy Harris doing quite a lot of the work on Carla's lip.'

'Point taken, but I'm not trying to steal Cy's thunder—far from it. He's the best anatomist I've ever known, including my professor at Oxford. Carla's lip was a miracle of reconstruction and he didn't use a single implant. I've learned a lot from Cy and I'm grateful. By the way, Carla is off to the south of France on holiday with her parents. It will be almost the first time the poor kid has been outside her own door. She even had a private tutor to teach her because she couldn't face going to school.'

Alison blinked back the tears that threatened to flow. 'Oh, poor Carla! Isn't it awful how a disfigurement can cause so much pain?'

Tom agreed. 'That's what my job is all about,' he said. 'It isn't always actual disease which cripples a person and poisons their whole life.'

Alison nodded, glancing at her watch as she did so. 'Heavens, look at the time. I should have been down in Intensive Care half an hour ago.'

Tom swung easily to his feet, colliding with Alison, who was starting to walk towards the door. He caught her, preventing her from stumbling, and Alison felt his face in her hair.

'Mm. You smell good.'

'So do all the other girls who use the same shampoo and soap as I do.'

Alison was trying to extricate herself from his arms when Greg walked into the room. She stiffened, her cheeks flaring bright red and her stomach churning, as she noticed his black look.

'Greg. I thought you were in London all afternoon?'

'So I see.' He glared at Tom. 'Sorry to break up this tender scene, but I have to get something from my files.'

Alison stepped forward. 'Tom only dropped in for a cup of coffee, Greg. And I worked right through the lunch-break. He was only in here for ten minutes.'

Greg frowned. 'I'm glad to hear it, but I wish you would do your courting in your own time. It could have been anyone who walked in just then.'

Alison shrank inwardly. Why did Greg have to come in just at that particular moment?

Tom intervened. 'Cut out the insinuations, Verney. It was perfectly innocent. It all happened just as Alison told you.'

Greg's face went white with anger. 'I'll thank you to keep out of this office in future,' he said. 'Alison has quite enough work without acting as your tea-girl, Saunders.'

Alison cringed as Tom clenched his fists and stepped forward, then felt relief as he obviously thought better of tangling with Greg and turned to her and smiled. 'Thanks for the coffee, Alison. I'll see you later.' He turned and, without so much as a glance in Greg's direction, left the office.

Alison felt sick. She looked in despair at the back of Greg's dark head as he bent over the filing cabinet. He needed a haircut, she noticed. The thick dark curls were beginning to encroach upon his collar.

'Would you like a cup of coffee, Greg?' she asked, trying to make an overture of peace.

'Don't bother.' He continued to hunt through the file, even though Alison was sure that he wasn't really looking for anything.

'What are you looking for? Perhaps I can find it for you.'

He turned and looked up. 'I need the DHSS papers on heart research in the UK,' he said, his expression blank. 'I was half-way to London before I realised that I had left them here.'

'They're in the other file. I'll get them for you. You should have asked me in the first place.' Alison brushed past him, their faces almost touching, and rested her hand on his shoulder to steady herself. 'Whoops,' she said. 'Don't knock me down.'

To her relief he smiled, and her heart lightened as she extracted the file from the cabinet and handed it to him. 'I wish you and Tom didn't always quarrel,' she commented as she watched him put the file into his brief-case and snap it shut.

Greg straightened up with a sour expression on his face. 'Every time I see him he's hanging round one or other of the female staff. I don't think it's good for hospital discipline, do you?'

Alison laughed, remembering how Greg had once been with her.

'I've never worked in a hospital where that sort of thing didn't go on,' she said. 'And everyone knows that the surgeons are the worst. At least Tom isn't married, like some of them who think they are God's gift to women.'

The thought flashed through her mind that Greg might be jealous of Tom's attention to her, not wanting her to so obviously enjoy the company of another man. If so she was glad. It would be good for Greg to know that she could manage perfectly well without him, even if it wasn't true. She looked speculatively into his eyes, wishing she could read his thoughts, but his steady gaze gave nothing away.

He straightened his shoulders. 'All surgeons aren't like that,' he said. He looked down at his watch. 'Well, I must be on my way. How about dinner this evening?'

Alison's stomach turned over. She would dearly have loved to accept, but she recalled that Tom was coming round and it would be impossible to put him off without lying, especially as she had turned down his invitation.

'Sorry, I'm having an early night,' she said, longing to

say yes. 'Some other time, Greg.'

He nodded. 'Some other time then.'

'No Marcia this evening?' she couldn't help asking. It was common knowledge in the hospital that Marcia had been staying at the manor with Greg and his mother all week.

He shifted his stance, looking decidedly uneasy. 'No, she . . . she has to go to Paris on business. She goes quite often, as a matter of fact.'

'Nice for her. Or doesn't she think so?'

He shrugged. 'I suppose she enjoys it. As a matter of fact I haven't asked her.' He turned towards the door. 'I'll see you to the intensive care unit,' he said. 'Make sure they don't spend the whole afternoon drinking tea, won't you? Keep popping in to keep them on their toes. I want it finished, and quickly. See if the foreman can lend you a manual—it will give you an idea of what the system can do.'

Alison obtained a manual from the foreman and took it to her office intending to read it, but thoughts of Greg kept intruding themselves into her mind. Especially concerning his relationship with Marcia. That was certainly strange, she thought. Sometimes they seemed to behave as if they scarcely knew one another. She looked up as there came a light knock on the door and Angela Barnes appeared in answer to Alison's call.

'Can I see you for a minute, Miss Wood?'

Alison looked surprised and then remembered that her title was not Sister any more. She still wasn't used to being referred to as Miss. 'Sit down, Angela,' she said, noting from the redness round Angela's eyes that the girl had recently been crying.

Alison looked at her enquiringly. She had always been

prepared to listen to the problems of junior staff, however trivial they might be.

She waited for Angela to settle down and then smiled encouragingly. 'Now tell me what the problem is, Angela,' she said. 'I'm sure it isn't as bad as all that.'

'It's Sister Lewis. She keeps on picking on me,' Angela suddenly blurted out. 'Ever since I was sent back from Marley General she keeps on making unpleasant insinuations.'

Alison looked thoughtfully at Angela. So that was it. She recalled what Mary had told her that morning about the two housemen fighting. Evidently it had reached Sister Lewis' ears. There had been something else too, about Angela and Tom.

'What kind of insinuations?' Alison asked quietly.

Angela blushed to the roots of her blond hair. 'About . . . well, about me and doctors,' she said. 'And it isn't true. I did flirt with those doctors over at Marley, but they were hanging around me all the time and I didn't realise they were taking it seriously. They had a fight and one of them got a black eye.' She had the grace to smile. 'Of course it went all around Marley in no time at all and they sent me back here. But I swear it wasn't my fault.'

Alison suppressed the smile that she felt rising to her face. 'I expect it will soon blow over, Angela,' she said. 'The great thing is to learn by the experience. After all, no great harm was done, was it? And hospital gossip is a very fickle thing.'

'Yes, I know, but it isn't the talk, it's Sister Lewis. Mr Saunders spoke to me the other day and she nearly blew my head off in front of the others after he'd gone. And the way she hangs around him fluttering her eyelashes . . .'

There was a short silence before Alison spoke. 'Angela, are you asking for my advice or are you just looking for a shoulder to cry on?'

Angela looked distraught, almost on the verge of tears as she said, 'I really came to ask you if you would give me a reference. You see, I can't stand it any more. I'm leaving Parkleigh as soon as I can find another job. I told you how things are now because I wanted you to know why I am leaving.' Angela's lip trembled. 'Only I've always been so happy here,' she said, finally descending into tears.

Alison was aghast at the news that her theatre, the theatre she had built into an efficient and happy team, was on the verge of complete breakdown. In a few weeks Sister Lewis had apparently destroyed something which had taken almost two years to put together. It wasn't just that Angela was leaving—nurses came and went all the time—but it was the reason for her going that was so disturbing. Added to that was the fact that Angela was the very type of nurse that Parkleigh could least afford to lose, for underneath her attractive, fun-loving exterior she was highly intelligent. It began to pass through Alison's mind that it might just be possible to get her transferred to the heart unit. After all, Greg had managed to persuade the Board to make an exception in Mary's case, so why not Angela if she was going to leave anyway? It would mean being overstaffed for a while, but Alison could see no objection to that. One or other of the new nurses was bound to leave for some reason—homesickness or an absent boyfriend, perhaps.

'Angela, I don't think we can discuss this sensibly unless you stop crying,' Alison said sternly, although in her heart she actually felt nothing but sympathy for the girl. 'I've heard that Sister Lewis is a strong disciplinarian, but she is extremely well qualified. Are you quite certain that you have made enough of an effort to work under her? After all, there are bound to be changes when a new sister takes over, and we just have to accustom ourselves to them.'

'I don't mind discipline, Miss Wood. And I enjoy hard work. You know that I always pull my weight when there is anything unpleasant to do. But Sister Lewis is catty and spiteful and I just can't take any more.'

'So your mind is definitely made up?'

Angela shook her head, causing her blonde curls to bob around her tear-stained face. 'I've asked to be taken off theatre duties,' she said. 'This week I've been working under Sister Webb and it is a completely different atmosphere, more like when you were there. But Sister Webb is coming into Cardiology next week, isn't she?'

Alison nodded. 'Angela, please don't do anything rash until I've had an opportunity to do something. I can't promise, but there is a very small chance that I may be able to get you transferred into Cardiology. I shall have to speak to Mr Verney about it when I see him. As you know, there was a rule that we shouldn't poach staff from Parkleigh, but we have a full complement of nurses now and I can't see any reason why an exception couldn't be made in your case.'

Angela's face became instantly wreathed in smiles and it passed fleetingly through Alison's mind that this was what she had been angling for right from the start.

'Oh, thank you,' she said. 'Do you really think that there is any chance? I'd be so grateful if you could swing it for me. You see, I don't really want to leave home.'

Alison rose to her feet. Angela was the daughter of a local GP and enjoyed a very comfortable life-style in a big Edwardian house on the far side of the town.

'I'll see what I can do,' she said. 'But now I shall have to ask you to leave. I really am rather busy. I suggest we leave the question of a reference until we see how things turn out.'

After Angela had gone, Alison sat thinking deeply. Something had to be done before Sister Lewis precipitated a serious crisis in the theatre, but the question was *what*. Strictly speaking, that side of the hospital was no longer under Alison's jurisdiction, Sister Lewis's immediate superior being Miss Hatherley, who was a dear but completely unwilling to get involved in anything that might cause unpleasantness. There was no doubt that if anything was to be done, Alison would have to take the bull by the horns and do it herself. It was a very delicate matter and not one to be undertaken lightly, since there could possibly be a public scene, especially if Sister Lewis was as spiteful and outspoken as she was reported to be.

But the more Alison thought about it, the more convinced she became that the best course of action was to have a quiet word with Sister Lewis herself over a cup of tea. It might very well be that she was so keen to make a go of her new job that she was completely unaware of the effect she was having on her juniors. Alison made a mental note to raise the question with Tom. He might have a suggestion that would ease Alison's task, for it was obvious that the coming interview with Sister Lewis was not likely to be a pleasant one. No one took kindly to being criticised, however mildly.

Alison was splashing in the bath when Tom arrived

that evening. She wrapped herself in a towel and ran to her bedroom window on hearing the bell and looked down to where he was standing.

'The back door is open, Tom. Oh, and make a pot of coffee and put a match to the fire, there's a dear.' He grinned and waved. Alison smiled back and returned to the bathroom. While she was adding some more hot water to the bath she wondered if Tom resented being domesticated. If he did, he didn't show it. The girls who regarded him as a debonaire man about town would be surprised to see how Alison treated him, though.

Downstairs, she found Tom lounging in an easy chair listening to Chopin. Before him on the coffee table was a newly opened bottle of vintage cognac.

'The coffee is perking,' he said. 'Meanwhile, I brought this to help the evening along.' He waved his glass before taking a sip of cognac.

Alison stood with her back to the fire, which was already beginning to blaze up the chimney. 'What time are you operating tomorrow, Tom?' she asked, eyeing the bottle doubtfully.

He laughed. 'Don't worry, I'm not risking getting struck off. Clea Daventry is due in theatre at two. Apparently she never rises before eleven and refuses to break the habit of a lifetime for the sake of conforming to hospital routine. It has meant revising all the theatre schedules though, much to Sister Lewis' disgust.'

'I meant to speak to you about Sister Lewis, Tom. What do you think of her?'

Tom shrugged. 'Not my type, actually. Nice legs though.' He ducked the cushion which Alison threw at him as she sat down on the sofa.

'You know perfectly well what I meant,' she said.

Tom thought for a moment. 'She knows her job,' he said at last, 'but I get the impression that our Sister Lewis isn't too popular with her staff. Too stand-offish in my opinion.'

'Except with the younger surgeons?'

Tom grinned. 'So you've heard about that! I wondered what this inquisition was leading to. Well, as I said, the fair Sister Lewis is scarcely my type, so you needn't worry.'

Alison bridled. 'Cheek,' she said. 'I don't care what you do, or who you do it with. Anyway, that isn't what I wanted to discuss.' She told Tom what Mary had said and how Angela had come to see her in her office that afternoon.

Tom raised his eyebrows at that. 'Could be serious if we lose all our best staff,' he commented. 'I had my doubts when I heard that Mary was coming over to Cardiology as well as you. Now I suppose it's inevitable we lose Angela Barnes, and she is one of the up and coming girls who will be hard to replace.' He paused, refilled his glass and then sat back and rubbed his chin thoughtfully. 'Before you do anything, let me have a word with Cy Harris. A quiet word from him may be enough. If that doesn't do the trick then speak to her yourself, by all means.' He stood up and came over to sit beside Alison on the sofa. 'Now, let us relax with some music,' he said. 'How about some more Chopin? It puts me into a very romantic mood.'

Alison slipped gracefully out of Tom's encircling arm and went over to her music centre. Soon the sound of the Nocturne in D flat major filled the room with its haunting melody.

Alison turned and smiled at him. 'I'll fetch the coffee

pot,' she said. 'Something tells me you're going to need it.'

The evening passed very pleasantly for Alison; the music, Tom's excellent cognac and the warm atmosphere in the room combined to produce a deliciously relaxed sensation. She was roused by her mother's chiming clock striking eleven and, lifting her head from Tom's shoulder, looked into his face.

'Time for you to be on your way,' she said.

Tom groaned. 'I never thought you meant it,' he complained. 'The evening is young still.'

'And I intend to have an early night, so I'm going to put you out.'

Tom kissed her gently on the lips and then stood up. As Alison rose to her feet she glanced at the bottle of cognac. Tom hadn't drunk a lot, but he certainly shouldn't be driving, she decided. She straightened his collar, which was rucked up, and brushed his shoulder where her head had rested. 'I don't think you should drive home tonight,' Alison said. 'Put your car in the drive and I'll ring for a taxi.'

Tom went to protest, but Alison lifted the bottle and waved it in front of him. 'Oh, all right, then,' he said. 'It's better to be safe than sorry, I suppose. I'll pick my car up in the morning.'

After Tom had gone Alison tidied the room and washed the cups and glasses before going up to bed. She lay awake for a while, thinking about Tom and making the inevitable comparison with Greg. Tom was nice. Whoever finally managed to tie him down would be getting someone rather special, she thought to herself. But for her he had none of the excitement that Greg could generate just with a glance or a word. She wondered where Greg had been that evening. Probably with some other girl, dining or dancing at one of the swish eating places with which the district around Parkleigh abounded.

Alison tried to concentrate on other things—on the events of the day, the work that lay before her tomorrow, but when at last she drifted off to sleep Greg's face was the last image that floated into her mind's eye.

The harsh jangling of the telephone by Alison's bedside jerked her into a confused consciousness and, half asleep, she groped for the receiver wondering who on earth it could be.

To her amazement it was Greg, his voice holding an urgent and concerned edge to it. 'I need you at the hospital,' he said. 'There's an emergency. Can you be ready in two minutes? I'll pick you up on my way.' There was a click as the receiver went dead and Alison was left with an awful sense of doom. It was her mother, it had to be. She glanced at her bedside clock. The time was a little after three. She hastily pulled on a pair of jeans and a sweater and reached the door as Greg's car pulled up in the road outside.

Alison's heart sank as she saw him glance curiously at the rear of Tom's Alfa Romeo before opening the door for her. Then she was caught up in the urgency with which he slipped the powerful car into gear and hurtled away along the lane in the direction of the hospital. Explanations could wait until later.

'Greg, is it Mummy?'

He nodded grimly. 'I had a call five minutes ago, just before I called you. I don't know how grave it is, but I thought it would be advisable to have you present.'

Alison's mother was conscious when they reached

her room, but was being administered oxygen from the regulated supply above her bed. Alison hurried to her side while Greg had a brief conversation with Bill Hemmings, the duty doctor who had thought it necessary to call him in.

Alison took her mother's hand, and her heart leapt when her mother turned her head and acknowledged her presence.

'How are you feeling, darling?' she whispered. She shivered as an awful fear gripped her when she felt how cold her mother's hand was.

Mrs Wood nodded feebly and sank back with her eyes closed. Alison looked for Greg, who was detailing the equipment that he might need. Bill Hemmings nodded and went hurrying out of the door.

Greg listened to her mother's heart with his stethoscope, a deepening frown on his face. Then he signalled to the nurse to wheel the ECG over to the bedside and applied the conducting pads to Mrs Wood's chest.

'It's right ventricle trouble,' he said to Alison. 'I've been worried about the possibility of this developing. The chamber doesn't empty properly and sometimes a pressure pulse builds up. Occasionally, as now, it leads to trouble.'

'Greg, isn't there anything you can do?'

He nodded as he examined the ECG. 'Several things, but the essential treatment at present is to keep your mother quiet and resting. Later I'll give her an intra-cardial injection to stabilise the heart action. And we'll keep her on oxygen at present to reduce the work the heart has to do to a minimum.'

Alison looked at Greg's tense face. He's more worried than he admits, she thought. She remembered the rela-

tives of seriously ill people and how calm and reassuring
she had always been with them. Even when there was no
hope left it was the nurse's duty to maintain confidence
and not to frighten people with an unpalatable truth,
however difficult it was. The suspicion came into her
mind that Greg was doing the same to her when in fact
her mother was dying.

'Greg, I think I have a right to know the truth. Is my
mother going to survive this attack?'

Greg turned to the junior nurse. 'Could you see if it's
possible for us to have a cup of tea, Nurse?' Then, when
the girl had gone he said, 'There is about a one in ten
chance of a cardiac arrest before the heart action stabil-
ises. However, I don't expect it to happen now, because
the ECG is slowly returning to normal. If we get through
the next hour I think she'll be fine.' He looked at his
watch. 'I think I shall phone Dallas and hurry them along
as soon as your mother is out of danger. You see, the
problem with these attacks is that once they start they
get more frequent. I take it your mother has never had
anything like this before?'

Alison shook her head. 'No. In fact recently she has
been quite a lot better.' She paused. 'When will you
operate?'

'As soon as I can get the valves. First thing in the
morning I shall alert the theatre for an immediate
emergency, day or night, as soon as Jason can get the
valves to us. We'll move your mother to London tomorrow. They have better facilities for dealing with this kind
of emergency there and, as I said, it will certainly happen
again.'

'Can I go to London with Mummy, Greg? I don't want
to be far away from her, not now. Not until the operation

is over and I know she will be all right.'

Greg nodded. 'I'll fix it for you to stay in the clinic,' he said. 'Actually it could be useful experience for you to see the working of a cardiological theatre at first hand. And it will certainly be appreciated at the clinic. They can always use another pair of hands.'

The nurse arrived with a pot of tea on a tray and placed it on a table by the window before withdrawing. Alison poured. 'Do you know, I can't remember whether or not you take sugar,' she said.

'None for me. I gave it up like any wise man. It helps the waistline too. I calculated I was eating two pounds of sugar a week so I decided that enough was enough—and I prefer my tea and coffee without it now.'

'I've never taken it. Mummy didn't, so she wouldn't allow me to take it. Not that I wanted to. I prefer to taste the things I drink.'

Alison looked at Greg and smiled. The conversation seemed almost trivial—*was* trivial—but it eased the tension in the room. 'Thank you for calling for me,' she said. 'It would have been so impersonal, just to get a call from the hospital to come at once and then the awful lonely drive, not knowing what I would find at the end of it.'

Greg's eyes didn't leave the ECG. 'There's a curious spike on the trace that I haven't seen before,' he remarked. 'The heart action is beginning to improve, though.' Then he looked thoughtfully at Alison. 'Sorry I disturbed you,' he said. 'But under the circumstances I thought it essential.'

Alison flushed, remembering Tom's Alfa parked in her drive and imagining what Greg must be thinking. 'I'm glad you did. It was very thoughtful of you.' She took her mother's hand in hers, and as she did so Mrs Wood opened her eyes and said something which Alison didn't quite catch. She bent her head down. 'It's Alison, Mummy. Don't be afraid. You've had a little turn, but everything is going to be all right now. Greg's here too. Would you like to speak to him?'

'I'd like a drink of water.'

Alison looked at Greg. 'Will that be all right?'

'Yes. In fact I think she can sit up. I was worried we might have a full-blooded heart attack on our hands, but that danger seems to be past now.' He looked at his watch. 'Nearly thirty minutes since the last flutter.' He helped Alison to raise her mother and together they gently laid her back on the pillows.

Alison poured a glass of water and moistened her mother's lips before allowing her to drink a little.

Alison glanced at Greg. 'What happens now?'

He stretched and stifled a yawn before glancing down at his watch. 'No point in going back to bed,' he said. 'I think I'll go to my office and catch up with some paper work. You know my extension number if you need me.'

'I'll stay here for a while, until Mummy is out of danger. Will you call in again before you leave?'

'About eight. I'll pop in and check that everything is all right before I go. Call me immediately if there is the slightest change in the ECG.'

Alison kept a wide-awake vigil beside her mother's bed. Her mother slept fitfully. Several times she woke, mumbled something incoherent and lapsed again into sleep. Once Alison thought she heard the words, 'I must be well for the wedding,' but it could very well have been something else and she smiled, thinking nothing of it. There was no wedding coming up in the family as far as Alison knew.

Her thoughts turned to Tom's red Alfa, parked in her drive for all to see. It had certainly compromised her in Greg's eyes—and perhaps not only Greg's, even though she lived in a lonely lane.

Alison shrugged. Did it really matter now that she and Greg had parted so finally? But in her heart she knew it did. It was terribly important to her that Greg should see her as she actually was. An absolutely straight girl who would never dream of sleeping around. A girl whom the breath of scandal, however slight it might be, could never touch.

She walked across to the window and watched the dawn break over the low, tree-clad slopes of the downs. Somehow she would have to find the words to explain the presence of Tom's car in her drive, although it was unlikely that Greg would believe her. If nothing else, it would set the record straight in her own mind. She wondered what it was like to make love, really make love, to a man you loved. The way things were going just now she was never going to find out.

As Greg drove Alison home the next morning after giving her mother a thorough check, he suddenly said, 'That was quite a fright your mother gave us.'

Alison glanced at him in surprise. 'You looked very much in control of the situation to me, Greg. Just how serious was it?'

'Quite serious. It could have gone either way. There are drugs I could have used and I would have been forced to as a last resort, but there is no way I want your mother on drugs at the present time. It could mean waiting for them to clear her system before I operate. I managed to get through to Jason Hunt in Dallas early this morning and he promises to have the valves here by the end of the week. In the meantime we shall go over to emergency nursing and complete bed-rest. Sister tells me your mother has been taking walks around the hospital during the day. I've definitely ruled that out from now on.'

'I didn't know that,' Alison said as Greg swung the car off the main road. The big 'Sold' notice in the hedge caught her eye again. 'I hope a property company hasn't bought the farm or I shall lose my field.'

'And what would poor Snowball do then?' Greg recited.

'It isn't funny!'

'Well you can relax. I bought the farm last week and I promise you can keep the field for as long as you need it.'

'Greg, you didn't! It's a gorgeous old Queen Anne house. I've been in love with it for years, but it is badly run down now. It will cost the earth to restore. And before I forget, thank you for letting me keep the field.'

'Well you can express your gratitude by making me a cup of tea,' he said.

'All right. And we can discuss the rent. At present I'm paying two pounds a week.'

'Riches indeed. I think we can forget any question of rent.' Greg changed gear with a flourish and brought the car to a standstill outside Alison's gate. Alison's heart turned over as he glanced into the drive and she saw his jaw tighten at the sight of the red Alfa. 'I see your friend is still here,' he said acidly.

'Greg I want to explain about . . .' But at that moment Tom appeared from behind the car and she fell silent as her heart sank through the floor.

Tom approached, smiling. 'I couldn't get the car

going,' he said. He stopped when he saw the grim faces looking out of the car window at him. 'Something wrong? I wondered where you had got to. It's not your mother, is it?'

Alison nodded. 'Everything is all right now, Tom. Mummy had a slight attack, but it's over now and she's out of danger. What are you going to do about your car?'

'I've rung the garage, they'll be along in a minute.'

Alison alighted from the car and walked round to stand by Tom. 'We can have a cup of tea while we wait,' she said. 'You too, Greg?'

Greg sat glowering at Tom before opening the car door and getting out. Alison turned to lead the way into the garden, but before she had taken two steps there was the sound of a scuffle and Tom went flying past her, ending up sitting on the grass verge holding his face, blood pouring from between his fingers.

Alison turned to see Greg climbing into his car with a face like thunder. Without a backward glance, he started the engine and drove away with his tyres screaming.

'What the hell did he do that for?' Tom asked as he climbed to his feet, his nose dripping blood.

Alison looked thoughtfully after the dark car as it disappeared round the bend in the road. She shook her head. 'I don't know, Tom. Perhaps you said something to upset him. Come on in. You need a towel and some cold water. I hope your nose isn't broken,' she added solicitously. But she felt her heart leap with a strange, unaccountable joy.

'He said something about my being careful where I parked my car,' Tom said, standing up and holding a handkerchief to his nose. 'I'd very much like an explanation from Mr Verney and I damn well intend to get one.'

CHAPTER FIVE

ALISON balanced the coffee tray on one hand and knocked on the door of Greg's office.

He looked up as she entered the room. 'Oh, good,' he said without smiling.

'Mind if I join you?' Alison poured the coffee carefully, stealing a glance at his expressionless face. Since the night of her mother's crisis, Greg had been almost entirely uncommunicative, except about matters concerning work, and Alison despaired now of ever putting the record straight about how Tom's car came to be parked in her drive all night.

A shadow of a smile crept over his face. 'Sure, sit down. I want to talk to you about your mother. Everything is fixed. Jason will arrive on Sunday and we will operate on Monday. I'm arranging to have your mother moved to London some time on Friday afternoon.'

Alison felt her heart lurch. Everything seemed so sudden and final now the actual time had arrived. 'Everything will be all right, Greg?' she almost pleaded.

He swept the stray lock of hair back from his forehead and smiled. 'I can guarantee it,' he said. 'Your mother is in far better condition to stand an operation than most heart patients. It should be a model operation. You'll go up with her?'

'Yes, I want that if it can be arranged.'

'I've fixed it for you to stay over the weekend. I don't want you to stay longer than that because the period of recovery in Intensive Care is rather critical and I find that the presence of visitors is often more of a hindrance than a help. But after the first week or so she should be fit enough to be moved down here. Then you can spend every waking minute with her if you want to.'

Alison laughed. 'No need to ask me. You won't be able to keep me away. How long will the convalescence be?'

'Six to eight weeks.' He consulted his watch. 'Well, since we are here together it might be a good opportunity to run over the work. Any administrative difficulties?'

Alison told him about Angela Barnes, impressing on him what a good nurse she could be while trying not to criticise Sister Lewis too harshly.

Greg listened with a deepening frown on his face. 'If that is the postion I can see no difficulty about transferring Angela,' he said. 'But the situation in the Parkleigh theatre sounds grave. Is Cy Harris aware of what is going on, or is he going to be suddenly presented with a serious crisis over theatre staff?'

Alison hesitated. Tom had promised to inform Cy, but any mention of Tom's name was like a red rag to a bull as far as Greg was concerned. 'I think he has been informed,' she replied, flushing slightly.

'I see. Well I think I shall have a word with him myself, just to make sure. What is this Sister Lewis like? One of the old school? Hard on her staff?'

Alison shook her head. 'She's quite young, actually. I think perhaps she is trying to impress with her efficiency, as it's her first theatre '

Greg rubbed his chin. 'I think the best solution all round would be for you to have a quiet word with her,' he said. 'If someone as senior as Cy Harris intervenes it will be all round the hospital in no time and her position will be impossible. Don't you agree? After all, she only needs to soften her attitude a bit. Why don't you give her some friendly advice? In the meantime I'll tell Cy Harris that you have things under control.'

Alison felt a shiver run down her spine as she realised that it would have been better to tell Greg right out that this was a case of female jealousy. Only pretty nurses like Angela had anything to fear from Sister Lewis. It was an age-old problem which often occurred where men and women worked in close contact with one another.

'I'll see what I can do,' she replied, wishing she had never become involved in a problem that was strictly speaking nothing to do with her.

'Good.' Greg stood up. 'Now we'll take a look at Intensive Care. I had a word with the manager in charge and he promised to put more men on the job.' He held the door for Alison and she sensed the nearness of him as she passed through.

Greg continued as he followed her into the corridor. 'The word is getting around that we are starting up and I'm having enquiries from all over Europe from doctors who want to place their patients here. It would be too bad if we were to be held up by the intensive care unit. After all, the theatres are almost ready.'

'But you are using the London clinic?'

'Yes, but I'm only allowed one day a fortnight in the theatre. They are already fully booked themselves. And this isn't the kind of surgery where a patient can be asked to wait for a few weeks. It is usually a matter of life or death.'

Alison glanced quickly at him. He had fitted her mother into one of his valuable operating days in preference to a patient who could have payed many thousands of pounds. There were no words, no way on the face of the earth, that she could ever repay the debt of gratitude she owed him. As for Greg's reasons for helping them, Alison felt as confused now as she had been at the start. It was true that Greg felt strongly protective towards her—he had proved that when he hit Tom—but since then he had been almost off-hand, which she felt was scarcely to be wondered at, considering the circumstances. And in any case, he spent all his spare time in the company of Marcia Dupont. Mary Webb had told Alison that Marcia was seen driving into the old farm and there were rumours that she and Greg would be moving in when they were married.

Alison felt a twinge of jealousy. She had loved the old house ever since she had been a child, and even now, although it was very dilapidated, anyone could see what a perfect family house it would be after restoration. Then there was Greg. Once Alison had idolised him—still did when she admitted the truth to herself—but there were too many barriers now. His mother's opposition to her, Marcia, Greg's opinion of her, her own pride and memory of the pain and humiliation she had suffered in the past . . . Alison ticked each one off in her mind, and taken together they seemed to stretch into a wide gulf which would separate her and Greg for ever.

Greg took her arm as they passed through the air-tight doors into the intensive care unit.

'How about lunch today?' he asked casually. 'I owe you a meal for all the good work you've been putting in since we've been trying to get this show together.'

Alison was taken aback. It was the first social overture Greg had made since taking her to dinner that first evening. She didn't quite know how to reply, although she had nothing on that day, having been intending to meet Mary Webb in the staff restaurant.

'I promise I won't bite,' Greg said, noticing Alison's hesitancy. 'And I can promise you a good meal. We'll go to the country club.'

'I'm sorry. Of course I'd love to come,' Alison said, looking down at her working clothes and thinking what a poor figure she would cut in the elegant surroundings of Parkleigh country club. Especially since Greg himself was dressed in a rather expensively cut light grey suit.

'You can call in at home and change if you would rather,' he said, reading her mind. 'It doesn't matter one way or the other to me.'

Alison smiled. 'I think I should feel happier,' she replied.

The intensive care unit looked very different from when Alison had last seen it. All the jumble of wire and the heaps of cardboard boxes were gone and technicians were already connecting imposing instruments to junction boxes on the walls.

'They *have* moved fast,' she commented.

Greg smiled. 'It only needed a word in the right ear,' he said, looking around him with satisfaction.

Alison listened while Greg explained the system to her in detail. Although immensely complicated, it could all be controlled by a single nurse seated at a central console. All the necessary information was stored in a computer memory and could be called up at any time by pressing a switch on a keyboard. Heart-rate, respiration, body temperature, even blood pressure, were all taken automatically and added to that, the nurse could observe the patient on a video monitor.

'It takes a lot of the load from the shoulders of the nurses,' Greg explained.

'It does seem rather impersonal, though. It seems to undermine the nurse-patient relationship to some extent.'

Greg nodded. 'There is that danger, but that's where you come in. Like all machinery it needs to be used intelligently, not in place of human contact, but to help it to be used in a more caring way. I'm not expecting our nurses to be sitting goggling into a television screen at patients all day long. I hope they will have more meaningful things to do than that. My intention is to provide the very best standard of care from the nurses and the doctors and surgeons. All working together as a team. That is why I needed you.'

Greg paused and his brown eyes rested on Alison's face for a brief moment. 'You set a standard of nursing care and competence, and you are a born leader. Where you show the way, the others will follow. There are no doubts in my mind about the nursing side of this heart unit, it will be the best. And it will be my job to ensure that the surgical side reaches the same high standard.'

As Alison looked up at Greg there was no question in her mind about his ability to do what he promised, aware as she was of his power and determination. Ever since she first met Greg she had wanted to stand by his side, but then it had been marriage she was thinking of. This was very far from second best, she decided. As Greg had said, they made a good team. Only a few weeks before, the heart unit had been an empty shell, just bricks and mortar. Now it was almost fully equipped with the best that modern technology could provide, and soon the staff of administrators would be installed to take the load from Greg's shoulders. Within a few weeks this intensive care unit would be bustling with activity and the theatres would be working at full stretch. It was an awe-inspiring prospect and Cy Harris had done well to choose Greg to head the unit. His name alone would be sufficient to ensure that the best young surgeons in the country would be eager to work at Parkleigh.

'Penny for your thoughts.' Greg touched the tip of her nose and to her joy the familiar lopsided grin crossed his face.

'They aren't worth that much.' Alison looked around her. 'I was just feeling happy that all this is coming together now. It's quite an adventure, isn't it?'

Greg put his arm around her shoulders. 'I knew you would see it like that,' he said. 'I feel that way too. This is my first real command. Now I know what it is like to be the captain of a ship—it's quite a sensation. I can't wait to show it off to Jason Hunt. He'll be green when he sees some of the equipment.'

Alison laughed. 'You're like little boys showing off your new toys!'

'Something like that,' Greg rejoined. 'But this is better. You've no idea what this place means to me. When I first heard that it was going through I was determined it would be mine.'

'And Cy Harris was equally determined that you should have it,' Alison said. 'Great minds think alike, it seems.'

Greg nodded. 'If he hadn't been I would have fought him for it.' He took Alison by the hand. 'I suggest we go to lunch,' he said. 'Everything here seems to be under control.'

They passed Tom in the main entrance hall. He came barging in through the door with an extremely anxious expression on his face. Alison noticed that his nose was still swollen and quite red, even though he had obviously tried to disguise the fact with talcum powder.

He waved to Alison, completely ignoring Greg's presence. 'Can't stop,' he said. 'My favourite patient is throwing a tantrum. I'll ring you later.' He disappeared into a lift.

'He must mean Clea Daventry,' Alison remarked.

Greg laughed. 'Yes, I heard he'd pulled her face rather tight, which apparently didn't suit her ladyship at all. I think she's been asking for a second opinion.'

'Face-lifts are always tight at first. In a couple of weeks she'll be delighted and praising Tom to the heavens. He really is a very good plastic surgeon, you know.'

Greg gave a non-committal grunt which made Alison glance at him nervously. One look at Tom had caused his earlier good humour to fly out of the window. Lunch, it seemed, was going to be a tense affair after all.

'Where's your car?' Greg asked, glancing at the space which had been allocated to Alison since her promotion.

'It's having a service. The tappets are very noisy and need doing.'

Greg raised his eyebrows. 'Don't tell me you know about engines too?'

Alison laughed. 'I don't know a tappet from a turnip. I'm just repeating what the foreman at the garage told me. Tom told me there was something wrong.' Alison could have bitten off her tongue as she noticed the scowl on Greg's face.

He sat tapping the steering wheel with the keys and for a moment Alison thought he was going to say something about Tom. Then evidently he changed his mind and slipped the key into the lock and, starting the engine, drove smoothly out of the car park in a brooding silence.

He hadn't spoken a single word by the time he pulled up in Alison's drive and it was beginning to irk her. Greg was behaving like a spoiled baby, Alison thought, beginning to feel indignant that he could have such an opinion of her. And there was certainly no need for this dog-in-the-manger attitude that he insisted on adopting.

She got out of the car and walked to the door, fumbling in her purse for her key. As she was fitting it into the lock she turned to see Greg following her and a devil seemed to get into her.

'Are you leaving the car there?' she asked.

Greg looked puzzled. 'Yes, why?'

'You don't think it might lead to talk if people see it parked there? I mean, they all know that Mummy is in hospital.'

Greg looked flabbergasted. 'What on earth are you talking about?' he asked. 'It's perfectly innocent.'

'Only you and I know that,' Alison pointed out, beginning to enjoy the situation. 'Other people might draw their own conclusions on seeing a man's car drawn up in an unmarried girl's drive.'

Greg shook his head. 'Not in broad daylight,' he said. 'They might if it were the middle of the night. But if it makes you feel happier, I'll wait outside in the car.'

Alison went inside, conscious that she had failed to make her point. Greg was determined to think the worst of her. Well let him, she thought as she changed into a green suit with a daringly split skirt which she had bought in Marley only the week before.

They were shown to one of the best tables in the restaurant, overlooking the stream which ran through the country club grounds. From a little bridge, people were throwing bread to the ducks, who were splashing and fighting over every morsel. Alison sat watching them with delight, ignoring the curious glances which had greeted their arrival in the restaurant.

Greg passed her the menu. 'I'll have the same as you,' he said.

Alison looked up and smiled. 'We are still on speaking terms, then. I thought you had gone off me, from the long stony silence.' She looked down at the menu, lost in the extensive selection of mouth-watering dishes. Alison had no intention of allowing Greg's ill humour to spoil her lunch.

'I'm having cream of asparagus soup followed by Lobster Timbale. Oh, and I want the lobster served with plain boiled rice, please.' Her face broke into a wide smile as she saw Greg's expression. 'Have you changed your mind about eating the same meal as me?'

Greg shook his head. 'Not at all. It sounds delicious. I was wondering what Lobster Timbale is, that's all.'

'It's boiled lobster served with a sauce made from sweet white wine and Grand Marnier. It's terribly expensive, but I wanted you to pay for being such a sulk in the car.' Alison looked defiantly across the table at him. She was not going to let Greg dominate her any more, she decided. There was no way she could win with him, but at least she could put up a fight.

To her relief he grinned broadly. 'I'm sorry,' he said. 'I suppose I was a bit terse, but that chap annoys me.'

'I think he's the one who should be annoyed, after you hit him like that. What was it all about?'

'There was something about his smug expression.' Greg looked embarrassed and called the wine waiter over.

Alison sat and looked at him. She wanted to hug him, to tell him that there was really nothing between her and Tom. But that would be stupid, she knew. Greg had to be made aware that he couldn't just come back into her life and take her over. The world had moved on and them with it. She fell to thinking about Marcia, wondering if Greg's mother approved to her. She probably did, Alison decided ruefully. Marcia Dupont had the same plummy accent as the Verney circle and very likely knew all the same people. She looked as if she would be at home in large country houses and would know how to handle servants.

'A hock suit you?'

Alison looked up to find herself being addressed.

'Mm, lovely.' A chilled hock was just right with lobster.

Greg leaned over the table towards her. 'I thought that after lunch we could run over to the farm and have a look around. I'd like your advice about some of the changes I intend to make. Nothing big, just enough to bring it into the twentieth century. Things like central heating, a swimming-pool—and it needs some extra bathrooms too. The present one is really ancient, with a gas geyser of all things! It would probably explode if I tried to use it.'

'I'd like that.' Alison was dying to see the farm. 'Are you going to keep it in period or have a mixture of ancient and modern?'

'Period. I think it would look sad otherwise. The trouble is there isn't a lot of furniture of that period on the market, not good stuff anyway, and I don't intend to furnish my first home with any old tat. There are a few Queen Anne pieces in the manor that I can take, but most of it is really too big for the farm.'

'Furnishing will be a headache, then.'

'Very likely, but I'm not aiming to complete it all at once.' He gazed quizzically across the table at Alison. 'Furnishing is really a woman's province. My own priority will be to get the farm working again—what's left of it, that is. The Woosters have been selling it off in small packages for years, just to make ends meet.'

'Well, that isn't surprising when you consider how bad Mr Wooster's arthritis is. That farm must have been like a millstone round his neck. He hasn't been near it for at least two years. He lives with his sister in the village ever since old Mrs Wooster died.'

Greg nodded. 'He still drives a hard bargain,' he commented. 'I had to pay the earth for it.' He shrugged. 'To tell you the truth, it wasn't a very good investment. But I just had to have the place and I couldn't stay in the manor with Mother for ever. For one thing, the place is so uncomfortable to live in.'

Alison concentrated on her soup, which was delicious. She knew enough about land prices around Parkleigh to realise that Greg must have paid a fortune for the old farm and it would cost another fortune to restore it, let alone fill it with antique furniture. Then she remembered that Greg did in fact have a fortune—several, if she included Parkleigh Manor with its thousands of acres of farmland and the shares in the family bank which he had inherited from his father. Last year, at the time of his father's death, there had been intense speculation in Parkleigh about whether or not he would give up medicine to concentrate on the estate. But Greg had put an end to that by putting everything into a trust managed by a close relative. Alison had admired him for it. Medicine was as much Greg's life as it was hers.

'This soup is delicious,' he said suddenly. 'I only hope the lobster is as good.'

'I'm sure it will be. This place is very highly regarded in eating circles, isn't it?'

'Do you eat here often?'

Alison had to laugh. The meal she was eating would come to more than her weekly salary. 'You must be joking, Greg!'

Greg looked surprised. 'I wasn't joking,' he replied. 'Surely your friend takes you out for a meal sometimes? Or do you prefer to entertain him at home?'

Alison flushed and an angry retort sprang to her lips. Fortunately the lobster arrived and she remained silent, concentrating on the meal and the delicious wine.

'I suppose I struck a sensitive area,' Greg commented, provocatively.

Alison's heart sank. Greg was obviously looking for a fight. She looked at him.

'If this is the way you want the conversation to go, I want to return to the hospital right now. I realise what you are insinuating and I just don't want to talk about it. What I do with my private life is my own affair. Surely I don't have to remind you that you abdicated any rights you may have had in that area a long time ago?' Alison matched Greg's angry glare with her wide blue eyes, her chin tilted defiantly, but inwardly she was quaking.

Greg shook his head. 'I don't know what to make of

you,' he said. 'I would have thought you would have had the sense to keep away from a man like Tom Saunders.'

'Greg, is this why you asked me to lunch? To argue about something which is none of your business and about which you know absolutely nothing? What would your reply to me be if I questioned your relationship with Marcia Dupont?'

He gave a strained laugh. 'It's not the same,' he said. 'I think too much of you to see you throw yourself away on a man like him. I think you should stop seeing him.'

'Well I'm not going to.'

He gave an angry snort. 'We'll see about that,' he said, and began to eat his Lobster Timbale in a stony silence.

Alison ate slowly, her appetite gone. She was trembling, although she had no intention of allowing Greg to see that he had upset her. She ordered a Peach Melba to follow the lobster, but left it untouched and sat fuming while Greg unconcernedly ate an enormous portion of apple pie and cream.

Men are so insensitive, she thought to herself. He deliberately set out to provoke me and now he is perfectly happy to have succeeded.

He looked up. 'Coffee, or shall we go straight on to the farm?'

'I don't want to see the farm.'

'Oh, you were pretty keen to see it earlier, I remember. What has changed?'

'You hadn't insulted me earlier, or my friends, come to that.'

'All right, then. We'll just have coffee. Shall we have it out on the grass?'

When they were sitting at a small table next to the water, Greg suddenly said, 'I didn't mean to upset you just then. It's just that I don't think you could be happy with a man who is always chasing women. I think it would be a mistake for you to get too involved with him.'

'Greg, we've been over all that.'

'No we haven't. And I feel close enough to you to feel concerned about you. I don't want you to be the subject of gossip, that's all.'

Alison glanced across to where a young doctor from the spinal unit was entertaining a rather pretty dark girl and, with a jolt, realised that she was Sister Lewis.

'I think my being seen here with you is far more likely to lead to talk, Greg. All the original speculation about us died down after I started being seen with Tom, but this is bound to make it flare up again. Sister Lewis over there is taking a very keen interest, so I dare say the news of our lunch date will be all around the hospital by the time we get back. And it will cause plenty of speculation, too. All eyes will be turned in our direction for the next week, looking for the next development.' Alison compressed her lips and gave a faint smile. 'You see how easily a girl can lose her reputation in a close community like a hospital.'

Greg turned and looked covertly at the other pair, who were sitting almost within earshot at a table by the bridge.

'That's one of the doctors from Parkleigh isn't it?' he asked. 'Do you know him?'

'Arthur Nichols. He's a surgeon in the spinal unit. He trained at that place in Buckinghamshire, I think. He's very highly thought of.'

Greg nodded. 'Stoke Mandeville,' he said reflectively. 'He must be good. Introduce me. I have to get to know everyone some time and it's easier away from the hospital. There's no time there to chat and get to know people. Come on, let's join them for coffee.'

Alison stood up and approached the other couple, realising at the very last moment that she didn't know Sister Lewis's christian name. Luckily Arthur Nichols realised and helped her out, introducing the other girl as Jean Lewis. Alison could scarcely escape noticing the open hostility in Jean Lewis's face as she shook her hand; neither did she miss the fluttering eyelashes and the flashing smile that were levelled at Greg. Evidently the stories she had heard about Jean Lewis had at least some truth in them.

Arthur Nichols was far from overwhelmed by Greg's reputation and the two men talked shop naturally and easily, helped by the fact that they had both been to the same school, Winchester.

Alison listened, enjoying herself immensely. She loved hospital talk. Now and then Greg drew her into the conversation and she gave her opinion without embarrassment, and was pleased to see that both doctors valued her views and took them seriously.

Jean Lewis was obviously bored with it and when Arthur Nichols began discussing one of his patients who had a heart murmur on top of his disc trouble, she stood up and walked on to the little bridge where she stood watching the ducks.

Greg looked at Alison. 'Have a word now,' he said, motioning with his head in the direction of Jean Lewis.

With a feeling of trepidation, Alison stood up and joined Jean Lewis on the bridge. 'It's a lovely day for the ducks,' Alison said, smiling. 'Look at that one there, half farmyard and half mallard.'

Jean Lewis turned to her with a cross expression on

her face which made her look quite plain, Alison thought.

'Did you have to break in on us like that?' Jean Lewis hissed. 'I was getting on well with him until you turned up.'

Alison was taken aback. 'I'm sorry,' she replied. 'But it is quite public here and Greg asked me to introduce him to Arthur Nichols.'

'So it's Greg, is it? I thought there must be something in it for you to have got that job at your age. You can't be any older than I am.' Jean Lewis almost spat the words out and then stood leaning on the rail looking into the water with a sulky expression on her face.

Alison kept her temper with an effort of will. She would get nowhere if she started an argument. But when she spoke again her tone was very much cooler. 'I've been asked to have a word with you about the theatre,' she began. 'There is a whisper in the hospital that some of the nurses are unhappy. Do you know why that is?'

Jean Lewis coloured. 'If you are speaking about that little tramp Angela Barnes,' she said hotly, 'I shall be glad to be rid of her. She does nothing but cause trouble with the male staff. I think there is something wrong with her.'

Alison paused. It was plain that she was wasting her time, but she tried again. 'And Staff Nurse Carter?' she asked. 'My information is that the unrest runs very deep and that it stems from your own attitude to the nurses. I always fround Angela Barnes very willing and hard-working, and as for Staff Carter, she is so placid that I thought nothing would ever upset her. Don't you think it would be advisable to soften your approach a little? I mean, good staff who can work well as a team are hard to find.'

Jean Lewis went white with anger. 'I'll run my theatre in my own way, Miss Wood. When I took it over I found the staff discipline almost non-existent. The nurses were doing anything they pleased. Some of them weren't even wearing regulation uniform, and some of them were on very familiar terms with the doctors. I thought it my duty to at least try to bring some semblance of order to the place.'

'I see.' Alison shrugged and looked down into the stream where the ducks were feeding on water-weed, bobbing down with their tails in the air. 'Well, if you ever feel that you need my advice in the future, my office door is always open to you. But my suggestion is to bend with the wind a little, Jean. All of us are keen to see you succeed and we are all willing to help you in any way we can.'

'I'm sure you all want to see me fall flat on my face. Well that won't happen, believe me. And when I want your advice I shall ask for it, Miss Wood.'

Alison turned away with a heavy heart. No wonder the nurses were in revolt, having to deal with Jean Lewis every day. It was clear that before long a real crisis would develop in the theatre, perhaps even affecting the patients. But one thing was absolutely clear. Things couldn't be left as they were. Someone would have to do something.

She told Greg of her fears in the car as they drove back through the lanes.

'I'll have a word with Cy,' he said. 'Leave it with me.' After a short silence in which he was evidently pondering over the problem, he said, 'It's odd. She seems such a friendly and attractive girl.'

'She is with men,' Alison replied. 'I think that's half the trouble. She is one of these women who wants to be the centre of attraction and sulks and is spiteful when her nose is put of joint by pretty young girls like Angela.'

Greg laughed. 'I thought all women were like that,' he remarked.

'Well that's where you're wrong. I'm not like that, for a start. And neither is Mary Webb.'

'I stand corrected, but then you are a phenomenon, aren't you?'

Alison raised an eyebrow. '*Am* I, indeed? A short while ago I was no better than I should be, I remember. Or had you forgotten?'

Ignoring Alison's protests, Greg swung the car into the lane leading to the farm. 'You misunderstood me,' he said. 'And in any case, I apologised for saying anything to upset you. You are beautiful and clever too. Doesn't that make you a phenomenon?'

Alison raised her eyes to the roof and said nothing. Greg was now in a very good mood while she was still smarting over the words that had passed between them over the lunch table. The car jolted over a cattle grid and into the rutted farmyard, surrounded on three sides by ancient barns while the beautiful Queen Anne farm house made up the other.

'Here we are. Let's go inside.'

Alison reluctantly followed Greg into a wide hall and stood looking at the extravagantly carved oak panelling.

'What do you think?' he asked.

'I used to come here to play with Mrs Wooster's granddaughter during the school holidays. I must say it looks rather sorry for itself now. Just look at all that dust.'

Greg ran his fingertip along a dusty moulding. 'It's all original,' he said. 'Worth a fortune, too. You can't buy workmanship like this nowadays.' He looked at her and smiled. 'Come and look around upstairs.'

Alison walked nervously up the creaking staircase, reluctantly clinging to Greg's arm. He led her into what was evidently the main bedroom and together they looked out of the enormous windows.

Alison gasped as she looked across a wide meadow to an ornamental lake framed with trees. Even in its present state of neglect, the view was breathtakingly beautiful, with the sunlight sparkling on the water giving it an almost magical quality.

She stood looking out in awestruck silence, imagining what it would be like to live in such a house and to wake to this view every morning.

Greg stood close behind her, looking over her shoulder, and when his arms stole around Alison's waist it seemed the most natural thing in the world to lean her head back against his hard shoulder.

'What is the building over there by the lake?' she asked, lifting her arm and pointing to a round structure with columns and a pointed roof half-hidden by the trees.

Greg moved his head to see where Alison was pointing and his cheek brushed hers, sending an electric thrill through her body. Any physical contact between them was sweet agony, Alison had discovered over the past weeks, but never before had he demanded this degree of intimacy. Alison felt his hard thighs pressing against her legs and trembled, feeling she had to escape from his embrace before her body betrayed the unwise thoughts which were racing through her mind.

'That's a gazebo,' he replied. 'It's rather a nice feature, isn't it? That one is a smaller scale version of the temple of Vesta in Rome.'

'The trees need clearing away so that it can be seen properly.' Alison wanted to move away, but couldn't. Her body simply refused to obey her mind. What was it about Greg that did this to her? Why him and no one else? In the total stillness she could hear her heart hammering and she flushed, thinking that Greg could surely hear it too.

'The gardens will have to wait until the house and barns have been restored,' he said. 'Fortunately the Woosters were never great builders so the place is in practically original condition. Marcia is quite an expert on the Queen Anne period and she has been in here sketching and measuring for the past two weeks. She loves the place. Well, it's a woman's house, isn't it? Perfect for bringing up children in.'

Mention of Marcia's name brought Alison back to reality. She took Greg's hands, removing them from around her waist, and gently twisting away from him.

'Let's go outside,' she said. 'I would like to look inside the barns. They seemed enormous when we were little.'

Greg took her into the largest barn and Alison stood looking in wonder at the enormous beams, each thicker than a man's body. 'Quite something,' she commented. 'What will you do with these?'

'The barns go back to the fourteenth century,' Greg told her. 'Built by shipwrights from Southampton from solid oak. As you can see, this one is big enough to hold a dance in, but I expect I shall have it converted into garages and stables. By the way, I meant to tell you. I've bought myself a hunter. Perhaps we can go riding together.'

'Oh, Greg, that's marvellous. What's it like?'

'He's a big brute, ex-steeplechaser. I thought I'd enter him in the point-to-points in the autumn if I can find time to ride the fat off him.'

'You won't ride him yourself?' Alison looked up into his face in concern.

Greg laughed. 'My weight would stop him dead,' he replied. 'No, but I thought you might like to enter for the ladies' race. If you think you can handle him,' he teased.

'I'll handle him, just give me the chance!'

'I know you can. I reckon we can carry off the cup if we can get him into shape.'

They walked out into the sunlight together.

'Where will you keep him, Greg?'

'I hoped you would let me put him in with Snowball. Your field is the only one with good fences at present. Naturally I shall buy all his feed and find someone to groom him and exercise him. And it will only be until I get organised over here.'

'That's a good idea. Snowball will be glad of the company. I know a girl in the village who will look after him for you—she's mad about horses and she might be glad to earn some extra money. She's at college in Marley studying catering.'

'Great.' Greg held the car door for Alison. 'What do you think of the house?' he asked.

Alison leaned back in her seat. 'Do I really need to tell you? It's the kind of house I used to dream about living in when I was little. In fact it's every woman's dream house, isn't it? Have you seen the walled garden? I used to climb over the wall to steal peaches when I was eleven, with my skirt tucked into my knickers.' She laughed.

Greg laughed. 'I remember you,' he said. 'A little tomboy with pigtails. You always seemed to be in the top of a tree.'

'What will you do with the garden?'

'Marcia says it would make an ideal place for a swimming-pool, with that high wall to keep out the wind.'

'Greg, you can't disfigure that beautiful garden with a swimming-pool!' Alison turned to him in dismay. 'There's a better spot just down from the terrace and it's a natural sun-trap.' She blushed furiously, realising that it was none of her business what Greg did with his own garden. She laughed. 'Sorry, I'm getting carried away. Before you know it I shall have the whole thing planned for you.'

'I'm glad you are interested. I certainly won't allow a swimming-pool to be dug in the garden if you don't want it. Anyway, that will be some time off yet. The house will take at least six months to get into shape, probably even longer than that. The builder says I shall be lucky to move in before Christmas.'

Alison settled back into the leather upholstery with an odd feeling of relief. Christmas seemed an age away on this spring afternoon and even if the rumours were true and Greg was engaged to Marcia, there was unlikely to be a wedding until the house was ready for occupation. She glanced at him. It was foolishness, she knew, but in spite of all the pain Greg had caused her she loved him so much she couldn't think straight where he was concerned. She lived for the times when they were together, working side by side. Even when he was terse—and that was most of the time—Alison didn't care as long as they were together.

'You are very quiet. Are you tired?'

'No, just thinking.'

'Happy thoughts?'

'I think so. Why?' Alison looked at him, curious to know what was passing through his mind. She had grown used to Greg's abrupt changes of mood. This was the old Greg, the bitter outburst over her relationship with Tom forgotten for the time being.

'It's just that I feel guilty about working you so hard.'

'But I enjoy working. Especially now everything is beginning to come together. We nurses are used to long hours you know, it doesn't bother us any more than it does doctors. I remember when I was working in a hospital in Birmingham that some of the young doctors were working an eighty-hour week. I expect you did when you were training.'

Greg nodded. 'But that isn't what I meant,' he said. 'How about taking a day off next week? There's an auction sale in a big house near Northampton and we could make a day of it.'

'Oh, what use would I be at an auction? I thought Marcia was the expert on that sort of thing?'

'Don't worry about that. Will you come? I can promise you a good day out.'

'All right. I'd love to. I've never been to an auction before.'

The car turned into the hospital entrance and glided to a standstill in the space reserved for the head of cardiology.

As they hurried up the steps, Greg said, 'I'll let you

know which day. It's either Wednesday or Thursday. Your mother will be well on the mend by then, so you can let your hair down.'

Alison was annoyed to find that Marcia was waiting for Greg in the reception area. She took her leave of them, meeting Marcia's enquiring glance with a smile which she was very far from feeling in her heart. Marcia smiled back, but without any apparent hostility towards Alison, although it was obvious enough that Alison and Greg had taken a very long lunch-break together. As Marcia took Greg by the arm and led him away, deep in conversation, a huge emerald and diamond ring flashed on her left hand and Alison was gripped by a sudden feeling of panic.

She turned away and walked rapidly towards the heart unit, using the internal hospital entrance instead of going outside and through the main doors. When she reached her office Alison's eyes were swimming with tears.

The file on theatre scheduling lay open on her desk and she turned to it. It had all been worked out on the main computer and she was beginning to feel doubtful about whether she would be able to operate the schedule with the staff she had available. They would need at least one more nurse, even counting Angela, she decided.

There was a knock on her door and Mary Webb came in.

'Thank goodness you've turned up. Where's Greg?'

'I think he's left the hospital. Marcia came and commandeered him. They left about ten minutes ago. Why, what is it?'

'Lady Verney turned up. She's waiting in his office now and she isn't very pleased at finding Greg absent.

Apparently he had a lunch appointment with her and someone told her that he had left with you. Will you see her?'

Alison blanched. 'Oh, my God.' She stood up. 'Mary, can't you tell her that Greg has left the hospital? Please?'

Mary shook her head. 'Sorry. She almost bit my head off when I asked her if she would like a cup of tea.'

At that moment the adjoining door leading to Greg's office opened and Alison wheeled round to see Lady Verney standing glowering at her. She turned to see Mary disappearing through the other doorway.

Alison swallowed hard. 'Good . . . good afternoon, Lady Verney. I'm afraid Greg is out this afternoon. I have no idea when he will be coming back, but it could be quite late.'

Lady Verney advanced into the office, her eyes flickering over Alison's pot plants and the open file on the desk. 'So I understand,' she said. 'But I wasn't waiting for my son. He apparently has no time for his mother. May I sit down?'

Alison hurried to hold a chair for her, and then retired behind her desk and sat down.

Lady Verney regarded her in silence. Then at last she said, 'I'm sorry to hear that your mother is so ill. We must all pray that the operation is a success.'

Alison gulped, not knowing how to reply. Of one thing she was sure. Lady Verney had not dropped in to enquire after her mother's health. That was just an opening shot. She wondered what Lady Verney's true purpose in speaking to her was.

'It has been very worrying,' she replied. 'But Greg is confident that the operation will be a success.'

Lady Verney nodded. Alison reflected that Greg's

mother looked very frail. Her steps as she crossed the room had been decidedly unsteady. Greg had been a late child, she remembered, and Lady Verney must be seventy now. Perhaps that explained her possessiveness and the fact that she was so keen for him to marry 'the right sort of girl' as she had put it so bluntly on the last occasion on which she and Alison had spoken. But even that didn't excuse lies and deceit and Alison felt that she would never hate anyone quite as much as she hated the woman who sat across the desk from her.

Alison hesitated before speaking again. 'What can I do for you, Lady Verney?' she asked.

Lady Verney leaned forward and placed an expensively tooled leather handbag on the desk before her. As she did so, Alison's eyes were drawn to the ornate diamond ring on her left hand, the stones arranged to form a lovers' knot. It blazed in a sudden fire as the sunlight caught it. Noticing Alison's interest, Lady Verney stretched out her hand, presenting the ring for Alison's inspection.

'It is beautiful, isn't it?' she said. 'And it has a curious history. It was taken from a Spanish treasure ship by a Verney who sailed with Drake and it has remained in the family ever since. It was made in Peru for the Infanta of Spain as a betrothal ring.'

The ring had an almost hypnotic effect on Alison. As she leaned forward to examine it, the huge blue diamonds flashed, splintering the sunlight into a million colours, and a cold shiver ran down her spine.

Lady Verney withdrew her hand and sat looking pensively at Alison. 'Ever since then this ring has been handed down through the family to the bride of the heir,' she remarked. 'On my death this ring will pass to Greg's wife, if he has one. Otherwise it will be held in trust until he marries. Rather a romantic tradition, don't you think? I remember the day that Greg's father first placed this ring on my own finger. I was just eighteen and newly married when his mother died after a fall from a horse. It was all very sad. I remember crying my heart out that day. Greg's grandmother was a very lovely woman. Only forty-five when she so tragically fell.' Lady Verney's eyes looked unblinkingly at Alison. 'She was very like you to look at,' she added, 'but of course she came from a very good family. Quite closely related to the King of Rumania.'

Alison blushed at receiving a compliment from so unlikely a quarter, even if it was somewhat back-handed. She shifted uneasily in her chair. 'Lady Verney, if you could come to the point,' she said. 'You see I have rather a lot of work to do this afternoon.'

Lady Verney nodded. 'The young are always in such a hurry nowadays,' she replied. 'When I was a girl life was more leisurely; we had time to sit and think. And of course, no well brought up woman would have dreamed of taking a job. Now, even married women with children work.'

'Would you like some tea, Lady Verney? Or perhaps you would enjoy sitting with my mother for a while? I'm sure she would be pleased to have company. I'll have some tea sent to her room.'

Lady Verney nodded. 'Perhaps that would be a good idea,' she said wistfully.

She rose with difficulty, holding the edge of Alison's desk to help herself. Then, as Alison came round to take her arm she seemed to slip and fall. Alison came round the desk to find her sitting with a dazed expression on her face and the suspicion passed through Alison's mind that Lady Verney had in fact had a temporary black-out. If so, it could be symptomatic of several widely differing conditions, all of them serious at Lady Verney's age.

'Are you quite certain that you will be all right?' she asked anxiously after she had helped Lady Verney back into her chair. 'Shall I ask Dr Bateman to take a look at you?'

Lady Verney waved Alison away. 'I'm perfectly all right,' she said. 'And I don't intend to be examined by a young boy. Dr McIntyre is my doctor and when I saw him last week he said I was as fit as a fiddle. Now, take me to your mother's room.'

Alison looked at her doubtfully. Dr McIntyre was well over eighty and should have retired years ago. She remembered that several emergencies at the hospital had been caused by his insistence that everyone who consulted him was perfectly well.

'Well come along, girl. Help me to my feet.'

Reluctantly, Alison complied with Lady Verney's request, but as Greg's mother had no difficulty in walking to the lift in quite a sprightly fashion she put the incident to the back of her mind and thought no more of it.

In the lift, Lady Verney looked up at her and said suddenly, 'What do you know of this young girl whom Greg has been seeing recently?'

Alison flushed scarlet. 'If you mean Marcia Dupont, I'm afraid I don't know her well enough to give an opinion, Lady Verney.'

'That's the girl. Greg invited her to stay at the manor for a few days. I'm sure I don't know what has got into my son. He must see that she is totally unsuitable in every way. A typical London girl. She even suggested that I convert the manor into flats and move into a cottage in the grounds.'

Alison couldn't help smiling at the thought of Marcia brashly telling Lady Verney how she should conduct her affairs. She wondered if Greg had told his mother about buying the farm. That would certainly upset her.

'I'm sure Marcia meant her suggestion in good part, Lady Verney. Perhaps she thought the manor too big and cold for you and believed you would be more comfortable in a smaller house.'

Lady Verney snorted. 'Nonsense,' she replied. 'The truth of the matter is, she has no conception of what it means to be a Verney. I'll tell you this; I would rather throw this ring in the lake than see it on that young woman's finger!'

Later that evening when Alison called in to see her mother on her way home, she found her full of Lady Verney's visit. Apparently her Ladyship had stayed on to have tea and the two women had got along well together.

'I can't understand why you and Lady Verney never got on, Alison. All afternoon she was saying what a lovely girl you had become, and how thoughtful and kind you are.'

Alison gave a rueful smile. 'Don't worry, Mummy. Marcia gave her Ladyship rather a fright, that's all. She'd soon change her tune if she thought there was the slightest chance of Greg and me getting back together again.' She leaned forward and kissed her mother on the cheek. 'I must fly, Mum. Tom is taking me to the cinema this evening to see *The French Lieutenant's Woman*. I missed it the first time round.'

CHAPTER SIX

ALISON SAT perched on the very edge of her seat, her finger-nails biting hard into the palms of her hands. She looked round at the crowded viewing gallery and then down through the plate glass window on to the floor of the operating theatre. It seemed impossible that the figure on the operating table was her own mother, or that it was Greg down there, swathed in green robes, his friend Jason Hunt by his side. And yet every screaming nerve in her body told her that it was so.

She should have listened to Greg. He had advised her to stay away, but Alison had insisted and he had given in reluctantly, arranging for her to sit in the viewing gallery in the company of surgeons and students from other London hospitals.

The scene on the theatre floor resembled something from a science fiction film. There were wires and television monitors everywhere and dominating the scene were the two heart-lung machines without which the operation would have been impossible.

Greg was working fast, his brilliance raising gasps of astonishment from the crowded gallery, but even so the operation had already been under way for over four hours. Occasionally Greg and Jason Hunt conferred, and when they did Alison's heart stopped beating until the operation was resumed.

Her head was splitting and the heat in the gallery was almost unbearable. She wanted to fly away, but she sat rooted to her seat, her eyes never leaving Greg's tall figure. There must be something wrong—it was taking too long.

The young surgeon sitting next to her whispered something to his companion and Alison strained her ears to hear. If something had indeed gone wrong, surely he would know? But he was merely commenting on an exceptional feat of surgery and Alison returned her gaze to the scene below her.

He leaned over towards Alison, never once taking eyes away from the table. 'Have you seen Verney operate before?' he asked her.

She nodded. 'I used to work with him,' she replied.

'Lucky you. This is the first time for me. I'm impressed, I can tell you. And the man who is assisting knows his stuff too.' He shook his head in admiration. 'Is it true that he is returning to England?' he asked.

Alison said that it was and he rubbed his hands together in satisfaction. 'Good,' he said. 'The Yanks pinch too many of our best men.'

There was a sudden flurry of activity on the theatre floor, causing Alison's pulse to race. 'What is happening?' she asked anxiously.

'They are restarting the patient's heart. Quite an anxious moment for the surgeons.' He glanced curiously at Alison. 'Are you involved personally?' he asked quietly.

'My mother.'

The surgeon took her hand and squeezed it reassuringly. 'Hold tight to me and don't worry,' he said. 'You don't need me to tell you that Verney is the best there is.' He looked into Alison's face and smiled. 'You're a brave one,' he said. 'I couldn't face this if the patient was a relative of mine.'

Alison's head began to swim. 'I'm sorry,' she said, 'but I think I may faint.' Greg had been right, she shouldn't have come. The strain was unbearable.

'Sit it out. It won't be long now. Already the heart has been restarted.'

Alison glanced at him. He was a blond giant of a man and his presence was enormously reassuring to her. 'You aren't English,' she said smiling.

'Allow me to introduce myself. Carl Langer from Munich. In England studying on a scholarship.'

'But you said *our* best men.'

He smiled. 'My mother is English so I don't regard myself as a foreigner in your country. If you still feel faint I would be honoured to escort you to the restaurant. They are beginning to stitch up—the operation is over.'

'What happens now?'

'Closing the chest will take an hour and then the patient will be moved to the intensive care unit to recover.'

Alison glanced round the gallery. Already the audience was beginning to thin out. 'I can't leave now,' she said. 'I must stay until the end, if possible. As a matter of fact I feel better already now the crowd is leaving.'

'Then if you will permit it, I will sit with you. You haven't told me your name.'

'Alison Wood. I work with Greg at Parkleigh Hospital. We are setting up a new heart unit there.'

Carl Langer entertained Alison with stories of his trips around England, and how he was planning to visit Scotland before returning to Germany. She only half listened, her eyes riveted to the scene below her on the theatre floor.

At last she saw Greg stand back from the table and look up at her, his eyes seeming to hold her. Beneath his mask she saw him smile and then he winked at her.

An inexpressible joy flooded through her body and she felt the tears pour from her eyes and ran unashamedly down her face. She felt that she had never known such happiness as this. Her mother was going to be well again and she owed it to Greg. He had been as good as his word and there was no way on earth that Alison could ever repay him. Her face broke into a smile. She could have sung out loud or danced around the gallery. Instead she flung her arms round an astonished Carl Langer and kissed him.

'Very nice,' he said, laughing. 'But I assume that it was meant for our eminent surgeon down there.'

'Oh, Carl! I'm so happy.'

'So I see. Perhaps I should take you to the surgeons' room where you can bestow your kisses on the deserving recipient?'

Alison blushed as she rose to her feet.

The theatre sister met them in person. 'Mr Verney has gone along to Intensive Care with your mother, Alison,' she said. 'He wants you to wait for him in my office. Mr Hunt will be along shortly.'

Carl turned to go, but Alison insisted that he stayed to be introduced to Greg and Jason Hunt. He agreed with alacrity. Meeting two such eminent surgeons was too good a chance to miss, he said smiling.

The theatre sister showed Alison into her office. 'I envy you the job at Parkleigh,' she said. 'Greg Verney is a dream, isn't he?' She blushed and then added quickly,

'As a surgeon, of course.' She laughed. '*And* as a man. I hear he is unmarried; is that really true?'

Alison said it was.

'Gosh! I'd have had my hair done if I'd known. I bet he sets some hearts fluttering down there.'

Alison was spared from answering by the arrival of Jason Hunt. He patted her arm. 'Don't worry about a thing,' he drawled. 'Everything went according to the book.' He turned to the others in the room and added, 'And I should know. I wrote the book!' He roared with laughter and sat down heavily in an armchair.

Alison laughed with him. Jason, as she had soon discovered when she met him, was given to making rather old jokes and then laughing loudly at them. He and Greg were as different as cheese from chalk, and yet they seemed to get along perfectly together. It had to be mutual respect.

'How about a cup of English tea?' he asked the sister. 'I'm hoping that if I drink enough of it I'll get used to it.' He laughed again and Alison stepped forward and introduced Carl Langer to him.

Carl began questioning him about some of the surgical techniques he and Greg had used in the operation and soon the two men were deep in serious conversation.

Alison sat back, feeling drained of energy and happy not to make the effort of conversation. She longed to see her mother, but that, she knew, was quite impossible, at least for the present. She wanted Greg to come, needing his reassuring presence even though she couldn't have what she really wanted, which was the comfort of his arms. She rested her head on her fingertips to ease her aching brow and shivered, feeling cold in spite of the fact that the room was warm.

He came in after what seemed to Alison to be an age, his hair glistening wet and clinging to his head, straight from the shower.

Alison smiled and stood up suddenly to greet him, and at that moment the whole room went spinning round and she fell to the floor in a dead faint.

She came round to find herself looking up into Greg's eyes, his arms cradling her head.

'What happened?' she asked him.

'Just a faint, nothing serious. It's little wonder after what you've been through. I told you to stay away.'

Alison rested her hand on his arm. 'Greg, I feel such a fool. After all the years I've worked in a theatre!'

He smiled. 'If you are a fool I only wish there were more of them in the world. Now sip this water very slowly.'

Alison took a sip and spluttered. 'I'm sorry,' she said. 'I tried awfully hard to be brave, honestly, Greg.'

'You are the bravest girl I know. Your trouble is, you don't know when to give in.'

Alison felt her body begin to tremble and she clung to Greg, holding him close. Dimly she heard the others file quietly out of the room, prompted by Jason Hunt.

When they were alone together Greg said, 'There's nothing to worry about any more. Your mother will make a perfect recovery, I promise.'

The tears flooded from her eyes and she clung to him. 'Don't leave me, Greg. Not for a few minutes, please.'

He stroked her hair, holding her enfolded in his arms. 'I won't leave you,' he murmured. 'Not as long as you need me.'

Slowly the icy coldness left Alison's limbs and she

began to feel better. 'What happens now, Greg?' she asked.

'We keep your mother here until she is strong enough to travel, and then transfer her to Parkleigh. That will be some time next week I expect, although it could be sooner. I suggest that you stay here until tomorrow and then travel up to see your mother in the evenings.'

Alison nodded and then turned her face up to his. 'Greg, you've been a darling. I won't ever be able to repay you, but thank you.' She raised her face and kissed him lightly on the lips.

He grinned, the familiar old lopsided grin that tore at her heart-strings, disappointed as she was that he had not returned her kiss. 'You don't owe me a thing,' he said. 'Just be a great head of nursing, that's all I ask for the present.'

'What's that supposed to mean?' Alison asked, snuggling closer into his arms and thrilling to the feel of his face in her hair.

'Nothing.'

'It can't mean nothing, can it?'

'It means stop being nosy.' He touched the tip of her nose with his fingertip and smiled. 'I think you are well enough to sit in a chair,' he said. 'I'll call Sister and ask her to make a fresh pot of tea for us.'

Alison made no attempt to move. 'I don't want to sit in a chair,' she said, like a truculent child.

'Oh. Why not?'

'Because I don't.' She rested her head on his shoulder, delighting in the warm masculinity of him. Because I love you, and I don't want to leave you ever, she thought to herself.

Greg grinned. 'You look well enough to me,' he

replied. He stood up and hauled Alison to her feet before depositing her unceremoniously in the armchair. 'Now sit quietly and I will find Sister.'

Alison watched him leave the room. She didn't want tea, she decided—she only wanted Greg. She wondered what he meant by 'for the present'. Her heart lurched. It could only mean one thing really, and that she would never be able to do.

She opened her purse and took out her small mirror to look at herself. She pulled a face. As she expected, she looked awful after all those tears, with puffy eyes and a red nose. No wonder Greg had wanted to get away. Marcia always looked immaculate and Alison was certain that Greg never saw her any way but well turned out.

She combed her hair with firm strokes and pondered over Greg's words. He had definitely intimated that something more would be expected of her than a strict business arrangement. There was so much about Greg that confused her lately though, like his constantly changing moods and the unexpected attack on Tom.

When Greg returned with the theatre sister, Alison was reasonably composed, with her hair neatly combed and freshly applied lipstick.

The theatre sister smiled at her. 'You'll feel better after a nice cup of tea,' she remarked as she put the kettle on. 'You've been under quite a strain, I can see. Still, it's all over now. I've been in to see your mother and she is as well as can be expected after a major operation. Better, really.' She glanced at Greg. 'Thanks to the skill of the surgeon there is very little post-operative shock.'

Alison smiled to herself. Greg had made another

conquest, although he seemed unaware of it, as always. She watched him cross to the window and look out on to the busy London street. He had the firm profile she had seen on old Greek statues in the British museum. What an actor he would have made—photogenic from every angle, a photographer's dream.

He saw Alison looking at him. 'Do I have a smut on my nose?' he asked.

'Something like that.'

They laughed together and Alison noticed the theatre Sister look at them with a puzzled expression on her face as she poured the tea.

In the end, Alison prevailed on Greg to let her stay another day in London, until Mrs Wood was well enough to be visited. Her heart had almost burst with joy as she had sat holding her mother's hand for a few minutes. Everything she had been told was true, and it was obvious that her mother was making an excellent recovery. Before Alison left she promised to come again in two days. Tom would drive her into London, she knew.

Greg pulled off the motorway at the first intersection, coming into Parkleigh along the back lanes past the church.

'Please stop, Greg. I want to go in.'

He looked at her as she unfastened her seat-belt. 'I'll come with you.'

'No, please. I want to be alone. I won't be long.'

Inside, the church was hushed and dim in the dusk, a single candle burning on the altar. The light seemed to draw her and she stood by the rail, uncertain of herself. Then she knelt and gave thanks for Greg's skill and her mother's recovery. For a long time Alison knelt in silent

contemplation. She had never been particularly relig-
ious, going to services only at Easter and Christmas, but
in the quiet little church a strange feeling of peace
seemed to enfold her, strengthening her. She stood up
and looked for a moment at the crests of the Verney
family which lined the walls and then walked quickly out
into the churchyard, disturbing a blackbird which flew
chattering up into the ancient yew.

Greg carried her suitcase into the cottage and seemed
reluctant to leave.

Alison remembered the cognac which Tom had left.

'Stay and have a drink, Greg. There's some very good
cognac. Surely you could have a little one?'

'Thanks, I'd like that.' He sat down on the sofa and
watched her put a match to the fire.

'Here you are.' Alison smiled, wondering what Greg's
reaction would be if he knew that it was Tom's cognac.
Men were such beautiful idiots. What would Greg think
if she suddenly leapt on Marcia and started pulling her
hair?

'This is superb brandy,' he commented.

'So I was told. I'm glad you like it.' She sat down
beside him. 'Would you like to listen to some music, or
watch the television?'

'I'll just sit quietly if you don't mind.' He looked at his
watch. 'I shall have to leave in a minute. I'm going back
to London this evening.'

Alison nodded. Greg's patients would always come
first. That was something Marcia would have to get used
to. Alison wondered if Marcia was really aware of what
it would mean, being married to a dedicated surgeon.

'Tell me what Jason Hunt thought of the heart unit.'

Greg beamed. 'He was pretty impressed. I don't

believe he thought we could do it over here. And when I told him about the research block he almost went green with envy.'

'Research block? I haven't heard about that myself.'

'A donation from my mother, believe it or not. She has sold some property she owns in Scotland and is endowing a research block as a memorial to my father. It's all signed and sealed—the architects are drawing up the plans.'

Alison drew her legs up under her. 'Greg, how exciting! What research will you be doing?'

'I'll be able to carry on with the new valve, and there are a few other ideas that I want to play around with.'

They sat, heads together, discussing his plans for the future of the heart unit, completely unaware of the passage of time. Greg told Alison about the research he had been doing before he left Dallas, and how he intended to carry it on at Parkleigh. The medical research council were interested in his work and would provide the money for equipment and staff. Alison was intrigued. She asked many questions, for most of what Greg said was far over her head, and he patiently answered her in simple terms.

The clock struck nine and then ten. Greg looked at his watch. 'I'll have to go,' he said. 'I was only going to stay for a few minutes, remember.'

'No time for coffee?'

He shook his head. 'You know what hospital routines are like. I shall have to break the speed limit as it is.'

Alison smiled. Sometimes she thought her whole life had been run to a hospital schedule. 'I know,' she replied. 'You'd better run along then. Give my love to Mummy.'

They stood at the gate in the darkness, listening to the low hoot of a distant owl, each reluctant to make the first move to leave.

'Greg, you must go.' Alison broke the silence first.

'I suppose so.' He gave a little laugh. 'It seems an age since we last stood here in the darkness.'

Alison shivered in the cold air. 'A lot of water has passed under the bridge since then.' She looked up at him. 'Go on. Be on your way.'

He moved towards her and his arms wound around her, pulling her close to him.

Alison struggled feebly, not really objecting, but nervous of her own feelings. 'Greg, please,' she whispered.

His warm lips met hers, softly at first and then, as her body quivered against his, harder. A flame seemed to leap inside her. Alison closed her eyes with a little moan and gave herself up to him.

When at last he lifted his head, the moon came out from behind a cloud. Alison looked up into his face, and what she saw written there made her heart beat faster.

'Greg, you must go now,' she whispered.

He put his head on one side. 'Don't go away,' he said, turning to his car. Then he lifted his hand. 'I'll ring you in the morning.'

Alison stood and watched the tail lights disappear round the bend in the lane and then walked slowly back inside the cottage, deeply conscious of a change in her relationship with him and feeling caught up in events over which she had no control. She closed the door and then walked into the sitting-room and sat on the rug in front of the fire.

She told herself not to be stupid. What she was feeling now about Greg was no different from what she had felt before, and that had ended in total disaster. He was attracted to her, there was no doubt about that. His kiss proved it. But in the end he would marry Marcia, not her. Perhaps, after seeing Tom's car parked in her drive, he thought she was easy, a plaything.

Her cheeks flushed with shame at the thought of being considered to be that kind of girl, especially by Greg. She rose to her feet, angry with herself for having allowed her body to betray her by responding passionately to his kiss. She had behaved like a moonstruck teenager and now she bitterly regretted it. The emotional upset of her mother's operation had clouded her judgment and she had followed her heart, not caring that in the past it had proved to be a very unreliable guide.

As she walked up the stairs to bed, Alison resolved to keep to her original plan. Her relationship with Greg must be strictly professional, with no overtones of social intimacy. Any other course was madness and would surely lead to unhappiness in the end. She trembled when she thought back to the wild dreams which her imagination had woven while she had been sitting with Greg. Marcia was no dream, Alison reminded herself, and neither was Greg's willingness to believe badly of her, or Lady Verney's implacable opposition to her as a prospective daughter-in-law.

The following morning, time dragged until just before lunch when Greg telephoned. Knowing it must be him, Alison hesitated to pick up the receiver, but when she did the news was good. Unless her mother suffered an unforeseen set-back, she would be transferred to Parkleigh at the weekend. Then Greg recited a long list of things he wanted done before saying a curt goodbye and ringing off.

Alison gave a rueful smile, remembering that his behaviour only a few hours before had promised much more than that. Then she shrugged. After all, she wanted a good, no-nonsense, businesslike relationship with him. Why, then, had it come so hard to realise that he wanted that too? Evidently the friendly intimacy of the past week had come to an end with her mother's operation.

The rest of the week seemed to fly by. Greg stayed in London, and since Marcia was absent from Parkleigh too, Alison surmised that they were staying together in Marcia's flat.

Every evening Tom drove her into London to see her mother, who grew visibly stronger every day. Alison hoped to see Greg there, but he was always absent during the evenings. Apart from his daily phone call he had totally disappeared from view.

Marcia turned up first. She appeared in Alison's office one afternoon and seemed surprised not to find Greg there.

Alison explained that he had been in London all week, attending to her mother.

'Damn,' Marcia said, banging her slender, jean-clad thigh with the thick roll of papers she carried. She looked at Alison. 'Sorry, I didn't mean anything. I'm awfully glad that your mother is well. When will she be home?'

Alison told her, all the time finding her eyes drawn to the enormous stones flashing on Marcia's left hand.

'That's wonderful news, I do hope it continues to go as well as it has started.' Marcia looked around, evidently undecided what to do. 'Look, could you tell Greg that these are the final plans? I have found a joiner to repair the staircase and make new window frames. And I am going to Paris for a few days and will be back some time next week.'

Alison nodded. 'I'll try to remember all that.'

'Write it down, there's a love.' Marcia smiled. 'I'm glad I don't have to cope with Greg all day,' she remarked. 'He's a most infuriating man, isn't he? Pity he's so damned attractive.' She laughed. 'Be seeing you.'

Alison watched her slim figure pass through the door, wondering why Greg, of all men, allowed his fiancée to go swanning off to Paris on her own. She picked up the thick roll of paper and weighed it in her hand before depositing it on a shelf.

When she turned round she found Lady Verney standing in the doorway leaning on her stick. She looked terribly tired. Alison ran to take her arm and sat her in the easy chair which Greg had insisted on placing in her office.

Lady Verney turned an anxious face up to Alison. 'I haven't seen Greg all week,' she said. 'I thought he might be in the hospital somewhere. I telephoned earlier, but the girl didn't seem to understand me.'

'Greg has been working in London all week, Lady Verney,' Alison explained.

'I see.'

Alison was overwhelmed with pity. Lady Verney seemed ill, although it could have been fatigue. 'Sit quietly and I'll make you a cup of tea,' she said.

'Thank you. You are a very kind girl, aren't you? I remember thinking so the other day.'

Alison gave a little laugh. 'Not really. I wanted a cup of tea myself. You can keep me company.'

'I was happy to hear that your mother is expected to

make a complete recovery—such a charming woman.'

Alison turned and looked at Lady Verney. Greg's mother was quite obviously in pain. 'Is there something wrong?' she asked anxiously. 'Lady Verney, don't you think I should call a doctor?' Alison thought swiftly. Both Tom Saunders and John Bateman were in the hospital, she knew.

'It's nothing, my dear. It will pass. It's just one of my heads.'

'Do you often have headaches, Lady Verney?'

'Recently, yes. I suppose it's my age. One of the penalties of growing older. I'll be quite all right.'

Alison poured the boiling water into the teapot and walked across to her desk to fetch the cups and saucers from the drawer. When she looked up she was appalled to see that Lady Verney was lolling sideways in the chair with her eyes wide and staring. As Alison watched, riveted to the spot, Greg's mother's stick fell from her grasp . . .

CHAPTER SEVEN

ALISON looked enquiringly at Tom as he beckoned to her to come outside. Fortunately he had still been in the hospital, pandering to the childish demands which Clea Daventry insisted on making on him.

'Is it a stroke, Tom?' she asked when they were out of the room.

He nodded. 'It isn't my field, of course, but I'd be prepared to stake my reputation that it is a cerebral haemorrhage. Quite a nasty one too, by the look of things. We'll have to move her to a room and get her to bed right away. I'll arrange for some porters to come with a trolley. And I think we should call in Walmsley from Marley Hospital, he's the best man around here. Oh, and get in touch with Greg if you can. I think he had better come immediately.' He paused. 'You'll need nursing help too. Stress to everyone concerned that it's quite likely that Lady Verney can hear and see everything that is going on around her. We don't want to frighten her any more than she already is.'

Angela Barnes was helping Alison to make Lady Verney comfortable when Jean Lewis walked in.

'I came as soon as I heard,' she said briskly. 'I've had experience of nursing cerebrals. Is there anything I can do?' She surveyed the scene and began to adjust the pillows, all the time talking to Lady Verney in a sympathetic, reassuring way.

Tom came in. 'Walmsley is on his way now,' he said.

Then, turning to Alison, 'Try to get in touch with Greg, Alison. Stress the importance of coming straight away.'

Before Dr Walmsley arrived, Lady Verney lapsed into unconsciousness and lay breathing noisily. Jean Lewis assured her that this was quite normal after a stroke and left to continue her normal duties, leaving Alison alone at Lady Verney's bedside.

Dr Walmsley arrived with Tom and carried out a brief examination.

'The left side of the brain is affected,' he said, after examining Lady Verney's pupils. He stood back from the bed and addressed Alison, speaking in a low voice. 'The only hope for a recovery lies in skilled nursing,' he informed her. 'The first twenty-four hours are critical and if her Ladyship can be pulled through the next two days following that, the chances of recovery are quite good. We shan't know what permanent damage has been done for at least three weeks after that. The essential thing is complete silence and no unnecessary movement. Any idea what brought it on?'

'Lady Verney told me she had been suffering from headaches for some time,' Alison said.

He nodded. 'A slow leak from an artery became suddenly worse. Even the slightest exertion can bring on a crisis under those circumstances. Has her son been informed?'

'We've been trying to contact him. I left a message at the London hospital where he has been working, but so far we haven't heard anything.'

'Well, I'll call back later this evening and if there is any change let me know at once.'

Tom looked grim after Dr Walmsley had left. 'Old

Walmsley isn't hopeful,' he said tersely. He shifted from one foot to the other. 'You're staying?' he asked.

'I must, Tom.'

'Perhaps Jean Lewis will stand in while you visit your mother this evening?'

Alison shook her head. 'I can't leave her Tom. Mummy isn't in danger now. I must stay here, at least until Greg arrives. Will you go and see Mummy and take that book she asked for? It's in my office.'

Tom looked worried. 'Are you certain that this is wise? Your mother is bound to ask questions and it will worry her if I tell her the truth. Jean Lewis will be perfectly able to cope here. After all, there's very little that anyone can do.'

Alison put her head in her hands. 'Tom, please! You don't understand. Please do as I ask.'

Tom sighed. 'All right, but don't let this turn into an obsession. Remember that you are a professional—you can't play God; none of us can.'

'Tom, I know what I'm doing.'

He shook his head. 'I'll go and see if Maintenance can put a carpet down outside this room to deaden the sound of footsteps,' he said. 'And I'll ring London again. Greg should be here.'

Alison walked as far as the lift with him. 'You think Lady Verney will die, don't you?' she said as they stood watching the indicator lights change one after the other.

He nodded. 'I'm sorry,' he said, 'but it looks like a bad one. Only a miracle will enable her to pull through now. Walmsley said as much.'

Greg arrived from London at a little after six.

Alison rose from her chair. 'Greg I'm so sorry.' She explained what had happened.

Greg looked at his mother, took her pulse and then straightened up. 'When is Walmsley coming again?' he asked.

'He said to call him as soon as you arrived.'

'The receptionist can see to that. Has there been any change?'

Alison shook her head.

'I don't suppose there will be for a few days. Did Walmsley give her anything to lower the blood pressure?'

'I don't think so. No . . . In fact I'm sure he didn't.'

Greg scribbled a name on a piece of paper. 'See if the pharmacist has any of this. It's new, so he'll probably have to go to Marley for it, if not further afield. Insist that he gets some, though.' He looked at Alison. 'Shouldn't you be on your way to see your mother?'

'I thought I should stay.'

'Well I think it would be better if you went to London. Tom Saunders is waiting for you in Reception.'

'But Greg . . .'

'Alison, I know how you feel, but there is a limit to how much one human being can do. Sister Lewis is coming in for the evening.' Then he smiled. 'By the way, you'll be happy to know that I'm transferring your mother down here tomorrow. I think she is getting rather restless.'

'Shall I prepare a room in Intensive Care?'

'No, I think we can put her straight into the main hospital. She really has made an amazing recovery from the operation. Some patients are in Intensive Care for a fortnight after a valve replacement.'

In other circumstances Alison would have leapt with

joy, but now her elation was completely overshadowed by the figure in the bed. 'Greg, you will allow me to help nurse your mother?'

'If you rest properly. We don't want any martyrs.' He looked Alison squarely in the eye. 'When I said you don't owe me a thing, I meant it. There are plenty of competent nurses in the hospital without you giving yourself a breakdown. Now relax, go and see your mother, and then go home and have a good night's rest. You'll be no use to me or my mother if you drive yourself too hard.'

Alison had to admit that Greg was right, but she felt an awful fear that Lady Verney would regain consciousness in her absence and ask for her. It was irrational, she knew. There was no reason on earth to suppose that Lady Verney would either ask for her or need her, but she couldn't get the idea out of her mind. She touched Greg's arm.

'Greg, I'm awfully sorry about your mother. I would do anything if it would help, you know that.'

She saw Greg's jaw tighten and her heart went out to him. Greg had never been very close to his parents, she knew. Little wonder, really, considering he had been sent away to boarding school when only eight years of age, but the pain he was feeling now was evident in his eyes.

'Age is an enemy that no man can fight,' he said. He rubbed his jaw. 'I'll stay here tonight,' he said. 'Spengler can ride down in the ambulance with your mother tomorrow. Now I'd better see about getting in touch with Uncle Henry and the family lawyers.'

Alison nodded. John Spengler was the anaesthetist who had attended her mother during her operation. She would be safe in his hands. She looked up into Greg's face, realising that he didn't expect his mother to survive until morning. Her whole being cried out to her to comfort him, to do or say something which might ease the pain. Alison gulped, choking back her tears, and turned away. She had almost reached the door when she remembered Marcia's message.

She turned. 'Greg, Marcia called in. She asked me to tell you she was going to Paris for a few days. I'm afraid she didn't leave an address.'

He looked at her, almost uncomprehendingly. 'Marcia?' he said at last. 'Did she say when she would be returning?'

'She didn't give a date. She left some plans for you to look at. They're in my office.'

He nodded. 'They can wait.' He glanced at his watch. 'You'd better run along.' He paused. 'Thanks for everything you've done. I promise to call you if there is any change.'

Tom was very quiet in the car coming home from London. Alison was glad to sit in silence, immersed in her own thoughts. To her amazement she found that her mother had been moved out of Intensive Care and into a room where Alison had found her sitting up in bed quietly reading some magazines. She had even been allowed out of bed for the first time since the operation, and was enormously pleased with herself and looking forward to returning to Parkleigh.

'Will you marry me?'

The question, coming out of the blue as it did, hit Alison like a thunderbolt, breaking through her train of thought.

'Tom?' She turned to look at him, not knowing what to say.

'I had intended to ask you over a candlelit dinner table, but now I find I can't wait until then.' He laughed. 'I told you I couldn't promise not to fall in love with you, remember?'

Alison's mind raced. Even though she had half-expected this, it still rocked her. She had come to accept Tom in the role of loving friend—but husband?

'I don't know what to say, Tom. So much is happening just now. I'm very flattered, but . . .'

'But you are in love with Verney,' Tom broke in. 'I'm not a fool, Alison. It is perfectly plain for all to see that you are absolutely dotty over him—but even you can see there's no future for you in hanging around Greg Verney. After all, he's supposed to be engaged to marry that girl who is doing up the house. What's her name? Marcia? Forget the past, leave Parkleigh and marry me. I know I can make you happy. I'll certainly try my damndest to. I've been offered a consultancy in London and I'm seriously thinking of taking it. I want you to come with me, as my wife.'

Alison sat quietly thinking over what Tom had said. It all made sense, of course it did. All week she had been toying with the idea of surrendering what had become a hopeless position and finding another job away from Parkleigh. To leave as Tom's wife was such an easy solution that she felt inclined to say yes straight away. She was quite certain that he meant every word he said, and with time the affection she felt for him might very well blossom into love—almost certainly would when they had a home and children to share. But for the rest of her life the memory of Greg would continue to haunt her. How would she cope with that?

'Tom, I can't give you an answer right away. Please try to understand how torn I feel. I owe Greg so much and he depends on me. There's the heart unit still incomplete and I can't just walk away from that. It's too important to me. I feel that it is a way of repaying Greg for all that he has done for Mummy.'

'You aren't just clinging to a foolish hope that Greg will change his mind and turn to you?'

'No—no, Tom. I'm not as stupid as that.' But even as she spoke, Alison knew that it had been becoming increasingly difficult for her to regard Greg as the man who had hurt and humiliated her in the past. Hers was a forgiving nature, and despite every resolve to the contrary she knew that in her heart she had already put the past behind her. Greg had been hurt and humiliated too, by what he had mistakenly believed to be her betrayal of him. He had lashed out viciously, believing that she had surrendered her virginity to a married man out of lust, and not love. Was there a man alive who wouldn't have behaved in exactly the same way? Alison wondered again if Greg knew the truth of it now, and then thought of Tom's car, parked all night in her drive. What a mess it had all become!

'I think I know what your answer will be,' Tom said suddenly, not bothering to hide the disappointment in his voice. 'But I'll still be around if you need me. Until I take up this appointment, anyway. And who knows,' he smiled and shot a sideways glance at her, 'you may come to your senses one day.'

Alison scarcely slept at all that night. Her anxiety about Lady Verney, the thought of having her own mother back on her doorstep again and the constantly nagging suggestion in her mind that it would be better to cut her losses and marry Tom, all conspired to keep her awake.

She rose at six, showered quickly and drove to the hospital in the early morning sunlight, her mind full of trepidation about what she might find, yet hoping against all the odds that Lady Verney would rally and pull through those critical first twenty-four hours.

To her surprise, she found Angela Barnes sitting with Greg's mother. 'Has there been any change?' she asked, looking across to where Lady Verney lay, the sound of her stertorous breathing filling the room. Alison shivered although it was warm.

Angela shook her head. 'She's been like this all night. Dr Walmsley has been in twice to see her, and Mr Verney is in his office now. He's been here all night. Jean Lewis has only just left—she was here too. She has been wonderful. I didn't realise what a good nurse she is.'

Angela flushed and looked confused. 'We had time to talk during the night,' she said. 'I think we just got off on a bad footing. Jean is very nice really, when you get to know her. I didn't know that it was her first theatre and she was keen to show how efficiently she could run it. I think most of it was my fault really. I was fed up because you had gone and I resented her taking over.' Angela hung her head. 'I'd like to try again,' she went on. 'I feel I'm letting her down by walking out now. You do understand?'

Alison raised her eyebrows, but she couldn't suppress the smile of pleasure that sprang to her face. Evidently Jean Lewis had taken her words to heart after all.

'Perhaps you would like to move into the heart unit later, when things have straightened themselves out,' she replied. 'And I am awfully pleased that you have decided to give Jean your support. I'm sure that it will make all the difference to her.' Alison smiled affectionately at Angela, glad that her original estimate of her had been right. Angela didn't only have beauty and brains, she had character too. She wasn't the sort to walk away from a situation because the going was rough or relationships hard to handle.

There was a low moan from the bed. Alison hurried over to find Lady Verney lying with her eyes open, her mouth struggling to form words. She bent her head low and just managed to catch her own name.

She turned to Angela. 'Fetch Greg,' she mouthed, conscious that Lady Verney might well be able to hear everything that was said.

'It's Alison, Lady Verney,' she said. 'Can you hear me?'

Lady Verney struggled to raise her head and then nodded feebly. 'Alison,' she said. 'Must have Alison.'

Alison took Lady Verney's left hand, remembering in time that her right hand might well be suffering the effects of the stroke, and squeezed it gently. 'You've had a little turn, dear,' she said, 'but you will be all right now we've got you tucked up in bed.' Her heart leapt when she felt Lady Verney's hand grip hers in return.

The old lady's eyelids fluttered. 'Is Greg there?'

'He's just coming. I've sent for him. He won't be long.'

Greg hurried in, moving silently across the thickly carpeted floor, his eyes taking in everything. 'It's Greg, Mother,' he said.

'Greg?' There was a long pause. 'Your father came to see me Greg.'

Greg's eyes turned to Alison and she noticed a deep sadness in them. He looked tired too, from staying up all night.

'Is Alison there?'

'Yes, Mother, Alison is holding your hand.'

'She's a good girl . . . I feel so tired.' Lady Verney closed her eyes.

'Greg, what can we do?'

'Ensure perfect quiet. No exertion or excitement of any kind. And pray. We aren't out of the wood yet by a long way.'

'Should Dr Walmsley be informed?'

'I don't think we need to trouble him yet. He will be coming in at about eight in any case. The only treatment at this stage is complete rest.'

'I feel so helpless.'

'All we can do is give her the chance to fight. Dedicated nursing care is the best treatment we can offer. You will stay, Alison? I mean, since Mother is responding to you, I think it would be the best course to adopt.' His eyes searched Alison's face. 'With luck she will regain full consciousness over the next two or three days and she seems to have confidence in you.'

'I'll stay as long as I can do any good, Greg. You know that. And perhaps you can arrange for someone to relieve Angela. She has been up all night.'

Angela came into the room at the moment. 'Excuse me, Mr Verney, but there is a man asking for you in reception. They couldn't use the telephone.' She looked at the bed. 'Sister Lewis had it removed yesterday evening in case someone rang this extension in error.'

'Very wise of Sister Lewis,' Greg said. 'I suppose you don't know who it is?'

Angela shook her head. 'He's a tall man, with greying hair. He arrived in a grey Rolls.'

'Sounds like Uncle Henry.' Greg smiled at Alison. 'Mother's younger brother,' he explained. 'Henry manages all the family affairs. It's best that he should be here.'

Uncle Henry called in briefly. A tall, erect man of about sixty, he subjected Alison to a long, cool appraisal when Greg introduced them, making her feel like an insect under the microscope, so close was his scrutiny.

'I've heard a lot about you from Greg,' he said. 'I'm glad we've met at long last, although I would have chosen happier circumstances.'

As he left the room in close conversation with Greg, Alison wondered just what Greg had told his Uncle Henry about her that made him so inquisitive. Probably it was just that the story of their parting had run round the family. There must have been a lot of family gossip when Greg left England for America. She liked Uncle Henry, she decided, especially since he and Greg seemed very close, like brothers really. Far closer than she remembered Greg being with his father, who had been rather a frightening figure. Very austere and formal, even with his son.

The day wore on. Alison's mother arrived early in the afternoon and was given the room just down the corridor from Lady Verney. Alison herself took the room between them, from where she could keep an eye on both of them, although her own mother was looking so well that it was hard to believe she had just undergone a very major operation. However, Alison had no intention of leaving the hospital now, not until Lady Verney's illness resolved itself one way or the other.

Lady Verney's periods of consciousness became longer, and although she was frequently confused in her mind and always called for Alison to sit with her, it became apparent by the fourth day that she was making a definite recovery.

By the end of the second week Lady Verney was so much better that Alison decided she could return to the cottage. By now, Greg's mother had an almost childlike dependence on her which Jean Lewis pointed out was not always in the best interest of the patient, even though it was quite common after strokes. Alison had come to respect Jean Lewis's opinion, and on her advice decided that it would be wise to taper off the amount of time she spent with Lady Verney. Alison would still have to feed Greg's mother, for she would take food from no one else, but the rest, the reading aloud and the long, rambling conversations, would have to be cut down. The trouble was, it would be difficult to persuade Lady Verney to accept anyone else.

Greg might be able to help there. It was time, in any case, to discuss his mother's future. Lady Verney still had a severe paralysis of the right side of her body and was going to need constant nursing if she was to make any further progress. But there was certainly hope. Only that morning Alison had noticed a slight stirring of the fingers of her right hand and her speech was quite definitely less slurred than it had been.

Alison decided to see Greg that afternoon and suggest he employ a permanent nurse for his mother, and there was something else too. Over the long hours spent at Lady Verney's bedside, Alison had thought long and hard about Tom's proposal of marriage and had made up her mind to accept it. It was only fair that Greg should be told that she was leaving Parkleigh as soon as possible, so that he could make the necessary arrangements to obtain a new head of nursing. Alison had decided to recommend Mary Webb, for she had been shouldering most of Alison's work as well as her own over the past two weeks, and was obviously fitted for the post.

There remained only the interview with Greg, for she could scarcely tell him news like this casually as they walked along a corridor. But the very thought of facing him caused Alison's stomach to churn with fear, and she knew too, that there was a real danger of her becoming emotional, perhaps even giving way to tears.

She went in to see her mother and found her sitting quietly by the window reading.

Alison wandered around the room, picking things up and putting them down again, uncertain how to broach the subject.

Her mother looked up. 'Why don't you sit down dear? You are making me feel nervous. How is Lady Verney today? Do you think she will be well enough for me to pop in later?'

Alison went and stood by the window, looking out over the lawns and flower beds and further, to where the herd of Friesian cows was grazing contentedly in the meadow. She gave a wry smile, remembering the day Greg returned and how she had compared herself to them. Then she had felt a need to be shaken out of her quiet little backwater, but that was before her whole world had been turned upside down—before the earthquake struck.

'I'm getting married, Mummy,' she said suddenly, not knowing how else to break the news. She looked at her mother, noticing the surprise in her face.

There was a long silence before her mother replied, but when she did she was smiling. 'Alison, that's wonderful news!' she exclaimed. 'It's high time you settled down and Greg is such a wonderful man, I've always liked him. I hope the wedding can wait until I'm on my feet again.'

Alison was thunderstruck. She had expected her mother to ask who her future husband was, never dreaming that it would be assumed that she would be marrying Greg. She sat down and took her mother's hand. 'I'm not marrying Greg, Mummy. Tom Saunders had asked me to marry him and I've decided to accept.'

She felt her mother's hand tighten on hers. 'If that is what you want, dear,' she said quietly. 'I'm sure Tom is a nice boy. I'm sorry for assuming the wrong thing. It's just that there have been times recently when I thought you and Greg might be getting back together.'

Alison slipped from her chair and sat at her mother's knee, resting her cheek against her hand. She had never told Mrs Wood the whole story of what had happened between her and Greg, but now it all poured out. She told how Greg had seen Tom's car parked at the cottage all night, and how Greg had attacked Tom the following morning.

'I wanted to explain, but Greg was so unpleasant that I couldn't bring myself to. God knows what he thinks of me now.' Her eyes filled with tears, which overflowed and ran down her face. She sniffed. 'Greg really does seem to have taken a dislike to Tom, and Tom doesn't deserve it. He's the kindest man in the world, despite his reputation with women, and he is never moody like Greg is.'

Her mother stroked her hair. 'I remember when I was

a girl, younger than you are now, your father knocked Jack Sibley down in the bar of the Swan on the night of the fair. All because Jack took me for a ride on the bumper cars. Poor Jack had an awful black eye and your father sulked for weeks afterwards. Men are so stupid when they are jealous.'

Alison had to smile, even though her face was wet with tears. 'Greg can't be jealous of Tom,' she said, wishing it was true. 'He doesn't want me, not in that way. All he thinks of is his precious heart unit. Even Marcia can't compete with that. It's all he ever thinks about.'

There was a noise from the direction of the door, and Alison swivelled round to see Greg standing there, watching her with a strangely questioning look on his face.

'Could you come?' he said. 'My mother is asking for you. Her lawyers are here and she wants you to tidy her up before she sees them.'

Alison rose hurriedly to her feet, wiping away her tears and wondering how much of the previous conversation Greg had heard. 'Lawyers?' she exclaimed in alarm. Surely there was no need for lawyers now that Lady Verney was making such a good recovery?

Greg smiled. 'Just one of my mother's little whims,' he said. 'She wants to have everything straightened out. I didn't see any harm in it as long as they don't take too long about it. Walmsley agrees with me that if it removes a cause of anxiety it can't do anything but good.'

Alison splashed her face in her mother's basin and washed her hands. As she left her mother's room she heard Greg ask Mrs Wood how she was feeling. Alison stopped in the doorway and turned to look at them as they sat together like old friends, her mother's face radiant and smiling.

Greg looked up. 'I thought you'd gone,' he said.

'I'd like a word with you, Greg,' Alison said. 'Privately in your office.'

He nodded. 'All right. Just as soon as the lawyers have gone. They shouldn't be very long.'

Alison slipped back into Lady Verney's room as soon as the group of men had departed. 'Come on, Lady Verney, you must sleep now,' she said. 'They've tired you out.'

'I'm perfectly all right.' Lady Verney lay back on the pillow with a faint smile. 'Now everything is settled,' she said. 'If the good Lord wants to take me I can die in peace.'

'Lady Verney, you will live for years,' Alison chided gently. 'Now, where is your cologne?' She touched Lady Verney's forehead and temples with cologne and took her hand. 'I don't want to hear any more talk about dying,' she said.

'I've been a foolish old woman, and I wronged you. You know that, don't you?'

'Lady Verney, please don't. You'll only upset yourself.' Alison felt herself very near to tears for the second time that day. It had been wrong of her to nurse Greg's mother, she was too emotionally involved.

'Have you seen Greg?'

'No, he's still with the lawyers. Do you want him?'

Lady Verney shook her head. 'They'll have plenty to talk about,' she said. 'Plenty to talk about . . .' Her voice trailed off and for a moment Alison feared the worst. Then the old lady's eyes opened again. 'Perhaps I should try to sleep. I feel very tired.'

'Would you like my mother to sit with you?'

She moved her head slightly. 'Yes, I would like that.'

Alison left Lady Verney in the care of her mother, informed the duty nurse of the situation and made her way to Greg's office.

Through the plate glass windows of the reception area she saw the lawyers gathered in a group around Uncle Henry as they carried on with their meeting in the car park. Evidently Lady Verney was right when she said she had given them plenty to talk about.

Greg's office door was open and Alison walked inside to see him looking out of the window, his hands thrust into his trouser pockets.

On hearing Alison enter, he swivelled round. 'What's all this nonsense your mother tells me about you leaving Parkleigh?' he asked at once.

Alison's knees turned to jelly. She walked unsteadily across the thick carpet and stood facing him. 'I'm marrying Tom, Greg. Did my mother tell you that, too?' She gulped.

He stood as if transfixed, his eyes narrowing dangerously. 'Rather sudden, isn't it? What brought this on?'

'Tom asked me to marry him the other evening and I told him I would think about it. Well I have, and I've decided to accept. Please don't make things more difficult for me than they already are.'

'You haven't told him yet?'

Alison shook her head. 'I thought you had a right to know that I would be leaving. I shall tell Tom this evening.'

Greg turned to the window and stood looking out and rubbing the back of his neck with his hand. 'I don't understand,' he said at last, visibly shaken. 'I need you here. The heart unit needs you. Only the other day you were telling me what a great adventure it all is. Now you tell me that you are prepared to throw it all up and marry a man you don't love.'

Alison flushed. 'I think that is my business, Greg. You have no right to make assumptions about my feelings.'

'No? When you were in my arms the other evening it wasn't Tom Saunders you were thinking about. You wanted me then, as much as I wanted you. It took every ounce of my will power to drive away from you that evening. And don't tell me you would have objected to my staying, because I don't believe it.'

Alison cringed inwardly. Every word that Greg had said was true. She wanted to confess that it was true and throw herself into his arms, but something held her back. There was still a barrier between them and Alison knew that she could never bring herself to cross it.

'I wasn't myself that evening, Greg. I think you are confusing my gratitude for what you did for Mummy with something else.'

'Gratitude!' Greg spat the word out as if it was poison and the anger in his eyes was frightening.

Alison backed away as he advanced on her. 'Greg, no.'

'What are you afraid of?' he asked.

His arms wound around her, pulling her close, and his lips met hers, more in anger than in love, but to Alison it didn't matter which it was. From the first light touch of Greg's mouth she was totally lost. Love and longing combined within her body to drive her on and she responded to him with a gentle moan of surrender. His passion rose to match her own, his hands pressing her close, moving slowly over her back while his lips explored hers in a sensuous caress.

Alison knew from that moment that she could never marry Tom, or anyone else—not while this mad obsession for Greg still had possession of her mind and body. When at last he released her and turned away, she burst into tears.

'Still grateful, I see,' he commented, mocking her.

His bitter words pulled Alison to her senses and anger welled up inside her. 'My God, you are despicable!' she said hotly. 'What a contemptible thing to say.'

He laughed at her. 'I'd say anything to stop you from marrying Tom Saunders.'

'Why? Why do you want to spoil my life, Greg? What exactly do you want from me? To stay here and work with you for the next twenty years until I'm a crusty old maid, a figure of fun among the young nurses? Is that what you want for me?' She stood facing him, her jaw set and her fists clenched into tight balls, her whole body quivering with emotion. 'There are times when I hate you, Greg,' she cried. 'If I were a man I should hit you.' She turned and walked towards the door, scarcely able to contain herself, bitter tears streaming down her face.

'I'm going home now, Greg, and don't dare to try to stop me.' She opened the door and as she passed through she turned and looked back to where he was standing with an incredulous expression on his face.

'Alison, don't go!' he called.

But Alison slipped quickly through the door, unwilling to continue the painful interview further.

With a few strides of his long legs, Greg caught up with her and, taking her arm, dragged Alison back into his office. Once there, he closed the door and stood with his back to it, watching her as she stood panting from her exertions.

She stepped forward. 'Greg, you must let me leave now. We have nothing more to say to one another. My mind is made up.' She trembled as she faced him, knowing that she had lied, but unwilling to back down under threat.

Greg's expression was black as thunder. 'I can't allow you to throw yourself away on a man like Tom Saunders,' he said. His voice carried an undertone of menace that made Alison quake in her shoes.

She stood her ground, looking him full in the face. 'Stop playing games. How could you possibly know what I feel or what goes on inside me? Aren't I entitled to seek happiness if I think I can find it?'

'Happiness, yes. But you won't find it with a man like him. A cheap thrill perhaps, like all the other girls he's been seen knocking around with.' He gave a harsh laugh. 'God, Alison! I should have thought you were far too level-headed to mistake a few nights of passion for love. Or are you no better than the rest, just a romantic little fool?'

Alison was speechless at this. Her breasts heaved with emotion. Greg had never before accused her of sleeping with Tom, his criticism of her being restricted to a few reproachful glances, and she felt physically sick that he could even begin to contemplate such a thing.

She turned away from him and walked slowly to the window. They had been over all this ground before and it was like turning back the clock and finding herself caught up in that last hateful scene with Greg. But then he had been torn by jealousy. He couldn't be jealous now, surely? His first loyalty had to be to Marcia. Alison shook her head, dismissing the thought that was trying to insinuate itself into her brain. Why was Greg like two people, one caring and wonderful, and the other cruel and vindictive? This was not the Greg who had given himself so generously to her mother, or comforted her after the operation. This man seemed almost like a stranger, and yet there was at least some truth in what he said. Just one kiss had proved to her that she could never marry Tom, not while Greg still had this impossible hold over her mind. But what was she supposed to do? Nurse an impossible love for the rest of her life? She bit her lip, feeling the tears begin to flow again, and turned to face Greg. He was standing watching her with a questioning expression on his face as if he expected her to say something.

'If that is really what you think of me, Greg, then I wonder you have any time for me,' she said simply, feeling totally drained of all emotion. 'Now can I leave, please?'

She felt hopeless, contemplating a future that stretched before her like a desert. Suddenly she had realised that the fears that had beset her when she first took the job had been realised. Soon she would become a hospital wife, worshipping Greg by day and returning home in the evening to an empty life. Alison felt at that moment that Greg had taken the one small chance of happiness that she had found away from her, and she hated him for it.

He came across the room and stood in front of her with his hands on her shoulders.

'You do see that I am right,' he said, his eyes full of anxiety. 'I was only being cruel to be kind. You do understand?'

'I only understand your words, Greg. I don't know anything about your intentions. I'm not a mind-reader. Now, can I go?'

'I can't let you go, not like this.' His voice sounded strangely strained. 'I'm sorry if I offended you. I only meant to make you see what a mistake you were making.'

'Then you should say what you mean, Greg, instead of insulting me. My relationship with Tom is absolutely nothing whatsoever to do with you—or had you forgotten?'

The chilling coldness of her voice surprised even Alison herself. She felt Greg's hands tighten on her shoulders before she was drawn into a crushing embrace.

'For God's sake, Alison,' Greg muttered hoarsely. 'Do you have to torture me like this?'

Before Alison could answer there was a light knock on the door and Marcia walked into the room.

CHAPTER EIGHT

Marcia looked at them in amazement, her hand still on the doorknob. 'Whoops!' she said. 'Sorry. Shall I go out and come in again?'

Greg turned to face her, his arm still around Alison's shoulders. 'No, come on in, Marcia,' he said. 'What is it?'

'Just a few more drawings. Can you see that the builder gets them? I can't stay long, Pierre is waiting outside in the car.' She walked over to Greg's desk and placed a large, flat cardboard folder down on it. 'I've done a few sketches to show what it should look like when it's finished,' she said. 'Want to run through them?'

Greg propelled Alison in the direction of the desk with a firm pressure on her shoulder.

'Come and have a look at the drawings,' he said to her. 'You'll be interested in these.' He looked at Marcia. 'Alison is in love with the farm house too,' he said.

Alison felt totally confused as she watched Greg and Marcia as they pored over the drawings. Surely Marcia shouldn't have taken the scene she burst in on quite so coolly? And who was Pierre? As she tried to collect her thoughts she glanced at the drawings.

Most of them were architectural plans and meant little to her, but the rest were very professional water colour sketches of what the farmhouse would be like when the restoration was finished. Despite her upset feelings,

Alison felt herself drawn to them. They were beautiful, showing the farm house transformed far beyond anything that Alison herself could ever have imagined. It was perfect and she found herself exclaiming with delight as Marcia showed her a view of the farm yard as it would soon appear, with a wide natural stone paving broken here and there by areas of cobbles surrounding the many trees.

'I'm trying to keep most of the trees,' Marcia told her. 'Especially the old walnut—it is such a beautiful shape and it frames a view of the barns from the dining-room windows.'

Alison flushed with pleasure, remembering how, when she was a child, she used to throw sticks up into the branches to knock down the nuts, and how she would walk home through the fields with her hands stained brown from the juice.

She caught Greg looking at her with a smile on his face. 'We must keep the trees,' he said. 'Even though the leaves will be a nuisance in the autumn. Oh, and before I forget, Alison doesn't want the swimming-pool in the walled garden, she has other plans for it.' He turned to Alison. 'Where did you say you wanted the swimming-pool?'

Alison flushed bright red at being thrust into the centre of the discussion, especially since Marcia turned the plan towards her and glanced up expectantly, a curious look on her face.

'This is a much better spot,' Alison said, indicating the place on the plan with a finger that shook noticeably. 'Where the garden wall meets the terrace steps. It's a natural sun-trap.'

Marcia studied the drawing and made a note with a

pencil. 'I hate to admit it,' she said, 'but you are quite right.' She laughed. 'You know the farm better than I do. I'll see that the drawings are changed and get in touch with the company who are installing the pool.' She glanced up at the clock. 'I really shall have to fly now,' she said to Greg. 'I'll be back to see how the builders are getting on some time next week. I'll give you a ring to let you know when.' She flashed a smile at Alison. 'I'm awfully glad everything has turned out for you,' she said.

Alison mumbled her goodbyes, her mind in a turmoil. Greg really was impossible. Everyone seemed to know what was going on except her. She turned to face him, still feeling angry and not a little foolish over the way Greg had tricked her.

'Perhaps you can let me know what is happening,' she said. 'I suppose it was your idea of a joke, to allow me to go on assuming that you and Marcia were engaged? Well I don't think it was very funny.'

Greg rubbed his chin. 'It wasn't very funny of you to tell me that you were going to marry Tom Saunders,' he said. 'All I was guilty of was letting you continue to believe what you assumed from the outset. I never once told you that Marcia and I were engaged, did I? In any case, I didn't believe you cared one way or the other. You never left me in any doubt that where you were concerned the very name of Verney was poison. Later, when I realised I still had a chance with you, it didn't seem to matter. It was all going to come out in the end.'

'I suppose you thought that you would make me jealous and then I would come grovelling at your feet. Is that it?'

Greg smiled, infuriating Alison still further. 'I didn't think of that,' he said. 'Would it have worked?'

'There are times when I hate you, Greg.' Alison's eyes blazed with a defiance that she was very far from feeling. Her knees trembled at the thought that her whole future lay in Greg's hands now. With a mighty effort of will, she maintained her attitude of outward calm. 'I have to leave now, Greg,' she said. 'I want to settle your mother down before I go home.'

He frowned. 'You've done so much for my mother,' he said. 'I'm sorry I haven't found the time to thank you properly. She could never have made such a good recovery without your devoted nursing. You know that, don't you?'

Alison smiled, relaxing at the change of subject. 'You don't have to thank me, Greg. The very little I was able to do, I did gladly. It helped to repay some of the debt my mother and I owe to you.'

'It was more than that. You will never know how much it meant to my mother that it was you who nursed her. You've no idea how much she needed your forgiveness.'

Alison gave a nervous laugh. 'It's strange how things turned out, isn't it? I thought I could never forgive your mother for what she did to us, and yet when it came to it, all I could think was that I desperately wanted her to live. In an odd sort of way I have come to quite like her.'

'You have a forgiving nature, Alison,' Greg said quietly. 'It's one of the wonderful things I've learned about you over the years. You're a very rare woman, my darling.' He smiled. 'Who knows, you may come to forgive me, given time.'

'For deceiving me about Marcia, Greg?' Alison walked over to the desk and picked up Marcia's water colour drawing. 'You are forgiven. It wasn't so very much after all, was it? Part of the fault was mine for leaping to conclusions. I really believed you were restoring the farm to live in after you were married. It never occurred to me that Marcia could be engaged to someone else, or that she is an architect.

She looked down at the drawing and studied it. Marcia's skill had brought the whole scene to vivid life and Alison could imagine herself walking in the shade of the giant walnut tree. 'You were quite right when you told me that Marcia had exceptional talents. She should be an artist as well as an architect. I love this drawing.'

Alison felt Greg close behind her, almost breathing down her neck as he looked at the drawing with her. A little shiver ran through her body and she felt that something indefinable, yet very wonderful, was beginning to happen.

'I wasn't speaking about Marcia,' Greg said. 'I meant all those hateful things I said, and the way I treated you.'

Alison put the drawing down on the desk and turned to look into his face. 'It's all water under the bridge now, Greg. I dare say you felt justified in saying those things. She smiled. 'But you do have an awful habit of acting first and thinking afterwards, you know. Like when you hit poor Tom, for instance. He never did know why.' She giggled at the thought of Tom's outraged face as he scrambled to his feet after Greg had hit him. 'Neither did I, for that matter,' she continued. 'Not unless it was a mistaken attempt to protect my virtue, and I can assure you that I am perfectly capable of doing that for myself.'

Greg smiled, and the old lopsided grin melted Alison's heart. 'My only excuse is that I love you,' he said. 'Don't you realise I can't think straight where you are concerned?'

Alison looked at him wide-eyed, not knowing what to answer. Greg's simple words were what she had been longing to hear for so long that now she could scarcely believe her ears.

'Don't you understand? I love you Alison. I've never stopped loving you for a second. I want you to give me a second chance.'

Alison turned away and walked over to the window, standing and looking out while her heart fluttered like a bird in a cage, longing to escape and fly to Greg. Her whole body was trembling and she crossed her arms across her breasts, not knowing what to say or do.

'Alison, will you marry me? I can't live without you, my dear. I tried, but it was a living hell for me.'

Alison turned to face him, allowing her arms to hang limply by her side. 'I don't know, Greg,' she whispered, her eyes filling with tears.

His face clouded as he came towards her. 'I meant every word I just said, Alison. I love you. I can't live without you.'

'Greg . . .'

The ring of the telephone seemed to fill the room with strident sound.

'Damn.' Greg lifted the receiver and listened, his eyes never leaving Alison's face. 'It's for you,' he said.

It was Angela. 'Can you come to Lady Verney at once, please, Miss Wood?' she asked. 'The physiotherapist is trying to persuade Lady Verney to be taken for a walk in a wheelchair and she refuses to allow anyone but you to take her.'

'I'll come straight away, Angela.' Alison replaced the

receiver and looked up into Greg's face. 'I must go, Greg. Apparently a crisis has developed. The physio can't cope with your mother. She is asking for me.'

'I'll wait, shall I?'

Alison shook her head. 'No, Greg. I think I need time to sort this out in my mind.'

He went to say something more and then checked himself. He smiled and picked up the drawings from the table.

'I have to go to Marley, anyway,' he said. 'I may as well drop these in to the builder on my way back. I wish you would drop in to the farm later. I think you will be impressed at the progress they've made.'

'Perhaps. I'll see if I have time, but there is an awful lot to do at home.'

He looked puzzled, but then he smiled and touched the tip of her nose. 'I warn you,' he said. 'You are going to marry me, so don't do anything stupid like promising to marry Tom Saunders.'

Alison smiled as an inexpressible joy flooded her body. She poked her tongue out at him. 'I haven't said yes, yet,' she said.

'But you will?'

'We'll see.'

Alison found a harassed physiotherapist trying to cope with Lady Verney. 'Thank goodness you've arrived,' she said. 'Her Ladyship is driving me right round the bend.'

On seeing Alison, Lady Verney became sweetness itself and immediately began to co-operate with them. Angela rolled her eyes and assumed a long-suffering expression, causing a smile to rise to Alison's face as she gently manoeuvred the wheelchair through the door.

'You really must try to co-operate, Lady Verney,' she chided gently as she propelled the chair along a tree-lined walk in the hospital grounds.

'I know, dear, but they don't really understand me. Especially that young woman who has been twisting my arm all afternoon. The other girl, Angela, is really quite sweet.'

'She was doing it for your own good, you know that perfectly well. Next week we shall start getting you back on your feet.'

'Well, I can't say I shall be unhappy about that, dear. And don't you think it is high time you called me Lavinia? After all, that is my name.'

Alison had to smile as she pushed the wheelchair into the shade of a tree and sat down on a bench beside it. 'I'll try to remember, Lad . . . Lavinia. Isn't the garden lovely at this time of year? When I get home I'm hoping to do some work on mine. I'm afraid I've rather neglected it this year.'

Lady Verney beamed. 'I knew you would share my love of gardens,' she said. 'Greg tells me that there is a lovely walled garden at your new house. You will let me choose plants for it?'

Alison didn't know what to say in answer to this. It was obvious that Lady Verney believed that she and Greg were to be married, and the idea could only have been planted in her mind by Greg himself. It was typical of his arrogance, and for a second the thought of totally denying everything passed through Alison's mind, only to be dismissed at the realisation that it would be upsetting for Lady Verney. The easiest course would be to go along with things for the moment. She glanced up to find Lady Verney looking at her and realised that she had been speaking to her and she hadn't heard a word, being deep in thought.

'I'm sorry, Lad . . . Lavinia.'

'I was just saying how important it is for a woman to have her own income when she is married. Women shouldn't be too dependent upon men. I never was dependent on my husband and I think our marriage was the happier for it.'

Alison realised that she had somehow missed the point of what Lady Verney had been saying. 'I do have my own income from my job, Lavinia,' she said in confusion.

'You don't understand, Alison. I'm sorry that I am not able to speak more clearly. I was explaining why I had to call in my lawyers. The reason why I have left half my estate to you is so that you will have an independent income.'

Alison was thunderstruck by Lady Verney's pronouncement. Without her knowledge the ground was being completely cut away from under her feet. Even half of Lady Verney's fortune must amount to a king's ransom, and there was no way she could accept it. She would have to speak to Greg about it as soon as possible. She glanced at Lady Verney, who was quietly contemplating the water-lilies on the ornamental lake, quite unaware of the bombshell she had let drop.

Alison shifted uneasily on the bench. She ought to say something to show her appreciation, she knew, but she didn't quite know what. An awkward silence developed which Alison finally broke. 'I'm awfully sorry, Lady Verney . . . Lavinia, but I really don't know what to say. You see, I've never been in anyone's will before.'

'You don't have to say anything, my dear. It's only

natural that I should leave my money to you. After all, I don't have any daughters to leave it to. You shall be the daughter I never had, if your dear mother will consent to share you with me, that is. Oh, and there is something else. We may as well get it all over with now. Will you pass me my purse?'

Alison's stomach churned with feelings of apprehension as Lady Verney reached into her purse, knowing what the something else was likely to be.

'I want you to have this now, dear,' Lady Verney said as she held out the ring for Alison to take. The sunlight caught the stones and as they flashed a million rainbow colours Alison stared at it, transfixed, feeling that she could never bring herself to touch it.

'Take it, dear. I can't hold it all day.'

Alison's hand shook as she took the ring from Lady Verney's hand and sat staring at it. The great blue diamonds seemed to symbolise everything she had hoped and longed for ever since she was little and had worshipped Greg from afar when he was home from school during the holidays. A tear started in the corner of her eye and trickled slowly down her cheek.

'I cried too, when I first held that ring,' Lady Verney said, looking at Alison perceptively. 'I think you are very like me at the same age, Alison. I just knew that you were the right girl for Greg and I nearly died when he brought that awful Marcia into the house. I had to tell Greg that she just wouldn't do, and she came from such a good family. I can't tell you how relieved I was when he broke off his engagement to her.'

Alison felt like breaking into hysterical laughter. So that was all there was to it? Greg and Marcia had plotted to show Lady Verney what marriage to 'the right sort of girl' might mean. That was why Marcia had suggested her scheme for turning the manor house into a block of flats.

Her heart flew free from the confining bands which had enclosed it for so long. She felt alive again, and tears of joy streamed unashamedly down her cheeks. She threw her arms round the astonished old lady and kissed her.

'I don't know why,' Lady Verney said, composing herself, 'but Greg set great store on your having the ring. He said I should give it to you myself, as soon as possible. Of course, I told him it would come to you anyway, but he insisted. He said it would show the whole family that we are reconciled. I wanted that too, so I agreed willingly.'

Alison sat turning the ring in her hand, half listening to Lady Verney, who was discussing the wedding arrangements.

'I thought that as you have no male relatives my brother Henry might consent to give you away, dear. Your mother was sure you would agree so I took the liberty of asking him.'

Alison gave a start on hearing that her mother had known all the time what was going on. No wonder she had assumed it would be Greg that Alison was marrying. Poor Mummy, Alison thought. It must have been a terrible shock to her when I told her I was marrying Tom. She picked up a stone and tossed it into the lake, wondering how she could get away to see Greg. She sat watching the ever-widening circle of ripples spreading across the water until at last they reached some baby ducklings who were swimming with their mother near the water's edge. Alison smiled as they bobbed furiously up and down and paddled frantically to the security of their mother's wing. The ripples Greg had made had tossed her all ways. If only she had known that he would be waiting to catch her and break her fall so gently . . .

Lady Verney was in the middle of describing the colour-scheme for the flower arrangements when Alison could stand it no more. She felt she had to be with Greg, even if it meant interrupting his mother's deliberations. She stood up and smoothed her skirt.

'Come on, Lavinia. I think you have been outside for quite long enough on your first day up. We can't have you catching cold. Besides, I promised to see Greg later, and I have to get ready.'

Alison settled Lady Verney down and then, taking the small bag which she had packed earlier, drove quickly home to the cottage. As she showered and changed, one single thought ran through her mind—to see Greg. Every second away from him was purgatory.

Her heart hammered furiously as she slipped a loose cotton dress over her head and fastened the buttons down the front. She had never dared to consider that her dream could come true. Even now, Alison felt that any minute she would wake to a cold reality, and she was afraid, afraid of losing everything again. If that happened now, Alison knew it would destroy her completely. She could never face life again, not without Greg.

Her Mini bumped along the rough track which led to the farm, the ruts made deeper by the constant passage of builder's trucks. Alison rehearsed what she would say to Greg over and over in her mind.

For a second, as she drove into the yard, Alison thought she had missed him, but then she saw his big car parked in the entrance to a barn and she breathed a sigh of relief. She parked her Mini between a pile of rubble and the rough bark of the walnut tree before running into the house calling Greg's name.

In the panelled hall she heard his voice from an upstairs room and she ran up the stairs two at a time, her footsteps ringing on the bare treads and echoing around the empty stairwell.

She found Greg standing by the window in the main bedroom and ran across the room to join him, linking her arm in his. Together they stood in silence, watching the play of sunlight on the water.

'Greg, you did have that undergrowth cut back,' Alison exclaimed excitedly, seeing the little temple clearly for the first time. Its reflection on the water danced in the ripples caused by a group of diving ducks. Alison leaned her head on his shoulder. 'It's like a corner of some Greek island with the sunlight on it.'

Greg smiled. 'I'm glad you came,' he said. 'For a while I thought you wouldn't make it. I was deliberating whether or not to come round to your cottage.'

'I've been taking your mother for a little stroll, the first since she had her stroke. Did you know they have managed to get some movement back in her arm, and she may even be able to walk again, given time.' Alison unlinked her arm from Greg's and reached for her purse. 'We had a little talk,' she said. 'Did you know that your mother was going to leave me all that money?'

Greg nodded. 'Of course I knew,' he said. 'She's been putting her affairs in order. You are to have half of her estate and the rest goes to her grandchildren, to be held in trust until they are eighteen.' He smiled. 'Our children will be quite wealthy, darling.'

Alison felt the colour rising to her cheeks as she replied, 'I haven't agreed to marry you yet. Everyone seems to be taking an awful lot for granted around here. Your mother is even planning the wedding. Don't I get a say in anything?'

Greg smiled and pulled her very gently into his arms. 'I think there has been quite enough talking,' he said. 'The only word I want to hear from you is *yes*.'

Alison looked up into his eyes, their faces so close that their breath mingled. 'There is something else,' she said.

Greg raised his eyebrows. 'Oh.'

Alison fumbled in her purse and took out the ring. 'Your mother gave this to me,' she said. 'But I can't take it from her, can I? It belongs in your family.'

'*Our* family,' Greg corrected her, kissing her lightly on the top of her head. 'It belongs in our family, my darling.'

'Greg, be serious. What can I do with it?'

Greg took the ring without speaking and glanced at it with a wry smile. 'There's only one thing to do with this,' he said, as he slipped it on to Alison's finger.

Her eyes filled with tears as his arms enfolded her, his lips warm and reassuring as their bodies seemed to meld into one.

Later, as they walked beside the lake in the last rays of the dying sun, Alison leaned her head on Greg's shoulder.

'I still can't believe it,' she said. 'Will you ever tell me what happened, darling?'

Greg's arm tightened around her and she closed her eyes, too happy, really, to care very much.

'I think you know most of it,' he said. 'I had to get everything right this time. I knew you would never agree to marry me against opposition from my mother. As it turned out she was already feeling terribly guilty about what she had done, especially since she had made enquiries and discovered that you were just the sort of girl she wanted for me. The only gamble was whether or not you still loved me.'

'Oh Greg, I never stopped loving you.'

'But you didn't answer the letters I sent, begging you to marry me. If you only knew what despair I felt. It wasn't until I learned that you hadn't read them that I realised I still had a chance with you. After all, you hadn't turned me down, so I knew there was hope.'

'I do love you so, Greg. If only I had known.'

'More than I love you?'

'Hundreds of times more.'

As their mouths touched Alison saw a sudden flash of fire from the ring as the last ray of the dying sun caught it. She closed her eyes in perfect happiness.

Doctor Nurse Romances

Amongst the intense emotional pressures of modern medical life, doctors and nurses often find romance. Read about their lives and loves in the other three Doctor Nurse titles available this month.

NO DOCTORS, PLEASE
by Lydia Balmain

"I don't want a *good* husband, I want a rich, exciting one." And with that in mind, Jenny Speed, whirlwind Staff Nurse of the Royal's private ward, has sworn never to go out with a member of the medical staff. By coincidence, so has gorgeous orthopaedic consultant, Gerard Sterne...

THORN-TREE MIDWIFE
by Barbara Perkins

When Staff Nurse Kate Raven takes a post as a midwife in Central Africa, she imagines that she has left her family troubles behind her. So she is not best pleased to find that handsome Dr Nicholas Kyle of Mutala Hospital is a cousin by marriage...

A DEDICATED NURSE
by Jean Evans

Gemma Lawson is a dedicated nurse — dedicated to the care of others because she cannot face the pain of her own past. But in Niall Barratt, head of St Vincent's trauma unit, she meets a man who has known tragedy himself, and overcome it...

Mills & Boon
the rose of romance